BLACK LIGHT: POSSESSION

L.K. SHAW

ISBN eBook - **978-1-947559-06-6**

ISBN Print - **978-1-947559-07-3**

BLURB

After relocating to Washington, D.C. to avoid an overzealous secret admirer, Dr. Madeline Parrish wants to learn all that the city has to offer. When a friend invites her to explore the dark pleasures at the exclusive BDSM club, Black Light, Madeline meets two enigmatic Doms, with whom she spends one explosive night.

Soon the love letters from her admirer start arriving, but now their tone is clearly threatening. When it's discovered the letters are eerily similar to those written by the serial killer, Cassenova, FBI Agents Joseph Crocker and Nathaniel Morgan are brought in to investigate.

Much to their surprise, Madeline is the sexy submissive they shared an unforgettable night with.

Crocker and Morgan tempt and seduce Madeline into becoming theirs. Casanova, however, has other plans for her.

Can the men catch the killer before he makes Madeline his next victim?

Black Light: Possession is a stand alone novel set in the Black Light world.

PROLOGUE

"And all I loved, I loved alone."
Edgar Allen Poe, Alone

MY DEAREST MADELINE,

From the moment I first laid eyes on you, I was entranced. There was this spark, this effervescence, about you that has only continued to grow. It's what made me fall in love with you. No woman could ever replace you in my heart. No woman could match your beauty. I lie in my cold, empty bed at night and marvel at the fact that soon you'll be lying here beside me, your warmth soothing me. Your beautiful eyes, lit up from the inside, stare into mine. The brightness of their violet depths reminds me of a glorious sunset. Purple is the color of royalty, which only seems appropriate since soon you'll be my queen.

I can't wait to run my fingers through your caramel-colored tresses. They twitch even as I write this at the thought of its soft silkiness against my rough hands. I want to see it splayed out across my pillow, its color a sharp contrast to the bright white of the sheets. Already I smell your favorite shampoo wafting through the air. It comforts me.

Then there are your lips. Their luscious plumpness tempts me like nothing else. The pink of your tongue as it darts out to just wet the surface has my thumb itching to rub across them and gather your moisture. Your flavor. I can only imagine what you'll taste like. I bet strawberries. My mouth is watering just thinking about it. Preparing for the sweetly tart flavor to burst across it. I bet your pussy juice is just as sweet and tart.

Fear not my dearest Madeline. Soon, we shall be together and you'll know the true meaning of love.

Until then, think of me.

CHAPTER 1

$\mathcal{M}$adeline

"For God's sake, not another one."

"You okay in there?" Sara, my assistant, called out from the waiting room.

I crumpled up the offensive sheet of paper and, with a sharp flick of my wrist, slammed it in the trash can on the floor under my desk. Stepping out of my office, I let out an exhausted sigh and dropped into one of the plush office chairs scattered around. I tilted my head back and closed my eyes, a throbbing beginning at the base of my skull. "I'm fine. Just another damn letter from my so-called secret admirer. I've lost count of how many I've received. I only know I'm so tired of them. I can't wait to get to D.C. and away from whoever this person is."

"I hate that some creepy stalker is driving you away." Her words were full of hurt. I peeked one eye open to glance over at her. She was shuffling papers around on her desk, refusing to look at me.

"It's not just that, Sara. I need a change of scenery. Things are… stagnant for me here. I'm not moving forward like I should be. Vince and I called it quits months ago. I haven't been to Eden to play since then. I can't bear to see him with another submissive. It's still too raw."

Finally, her eyes full of sadness, met mine. "You know running away from your problems never changes anything."

"I'm not running away per se," I replied sheepishly, because she knew I was lying.

"Your patients are going to miss you. You know that, right?" she didn't even bat an eyelash at trying to guilt trip me.

"Man you sure know how to hit where it hurts. I'll miss them too, but you know as well as I do they're going to continue getting excellent patient care from Dr. Sloane. You have to admit she even won you over, albeit reluctantly."

Sara sighed in frustration. "Yes, she'll be a great replacement for you, even if she's not you. I understand why you're doing it though. It's just that I'm going to miss you, Madeline. You're the best boss I've ever worked for. Besides, who else am I going to live vicariously through? All the talk of domination and submission really makes me want to try it out for myself. You're the only person I feel comfortable talking with about that kind of stuff. Both of which make me sound like such a selfish bitch."

"You're not being selfish. I'm going to miss you too, but over the last couple years I've felt this sense of restlessness. I'm thirty-six years old, and something is missing from my life. I just don't know what. I have amazing friends, you included, and up until a few months ago I had Vince. When it became obvious he couldn't give me what I needed, we grew apart. The shitty thing was, I couldn't even tell him *what* I needed. He'd tried everything, but it hadn't filled this… void inside me. I knew no matter what, I wasn't the right submissive for him."

Sara sat forward in her chair. "I know how hard the break up was for you."

I nodded. "I was devastated. It's my job to help people figure out what it is they want and need out of life, yet I can't even help myself. You know when those letters started arriving, I was actually a little flattered. I felt admired in a way."

I thought back to that first one. It was innocuous, bland even. Then they started coming more frequently, and I got creeped out. It wasn't long before I was getting a new letter a few times a week. Each one more graphic than the last, professing the admirer's love and devotion and how he couldn't wait for us to finally be together.

"I get it, and you know, even with all my bitching, I only ever want the best for you."

I rose from my chair and circled the desk, leaning down to give her a giant hug. "I'm so glad to call you friend, and you know I'm only a phone call away."

We were quiet for a moment before Sara broke the silence. "So, when's the going away party?"

~

FIVE HOURS LATER I WAS HOME AND CUDDLED UP ON MY COUCH after a long day of seeing patients. I'd just poured the last bit of moscato from the bottle when my phone rang. I smiled when I saw the name on the caller ID.

"Hey, G."

"You ready to take D.C. by storm, Parrish?" The deep, gravelly voice of my best friend soothed me in a way I didn't know I needed. I relaxed into the couch sipping my wine.

"I'm more than ready to see this new city of mine. The movers are coming on Thursday for all my stuff. I said goodbye to all my patients this week, so there's nothing more I need to do except head up there."

"I can't wait. I've missed your sorry mug."

I shook my head. Leave it to Garreth to give a compliment like that.

"I've missed you too." I cringed at the loneliness in my voice. Thankfully, Garreth missed it, since he continued without skipping a beat.

"You have no idea how relieved I am too that you're getting away from that town and whatever loser has been sending you those letters."

I stretched my neck from side to side to release the kink. "You've always been overprotective of me. Ever since I fully immersed myself in this lifestyle."

Through the phone I could almost see Garreth shake his head. "You were so reckless back then. A newbie sub who had no idea what the hell she was doing. I tried to warn you about fake Doms, ones who played the part, but were really just looking for an excuse to smack a woman around. Did you listen? Of course not."

"You have no idea how shocked I was when I discovered you were a Dom. I mean Trish and I were friends, and roommates, for two years, and I had no idea you guys were in the lifestyle. She never once hinted at it. Maybe because she was jealous of how seamlessly you and I connected."

Garreth groaned. "I tried explaining to her there was nothing between you and me. That you were like my sister, but she never believed me. It was what eventually destroyed our relationship."

I sipped my wine. "I figured that's why she ended our friendship as well. She didn't give me a reason, she just ghosted. In the end, I guess it doesn't matter. You turned out to be a far better friend than she ever was to me. Meeting you was the best thing to happen to me. I'm so glad you're my friend. And I'm even more glad that you and Hadlee convinced me to move to D.C. I'm so excited to see what the city, and Black Light, have to offer."

"The men here won't know what hit 'em. You're going to love this place as much as I do. When do you start work again?"

"I took two weeks off, so I've officially been on vacation for"—

I glanced at the giant antique grandfather clock I'd inherited from my mother—"almost six hours now."

"Perfect. I'll be over on Friday to help you unpack. Then we're going to play tourists, and we'll take you to see all the monuments and memorials. Saturday, Hadlee and I are taking you to Black Light. We'll get you a visitor's pass at the door. You'll also need to sign a non-disclosure agreement. I'll go over the rules of the house before we get there."

I shifted in my chair before taking another swallow of wine. "I don't know if I'm ready for that yet," I said cautiously.

"I can't believe you're going to make me talk about feelings," Garreth sighed in mock-disgust. "Look, I know you've been having a hard time since the breakup, but I think Black Light will be good for you. Find yourself a Dom to scene with. You need to release all the frustrations you're bottling up. It's not good for you."

There was the slight command in his tone at the end. Damn it, he'd pulled out the Dom voice. Even though we'd never scened together, he was too much like my big brother, my inherent submissive side couldn't help but obey, and he knew it, the jerk.

Still, I couldn't help but chuckle. "I thought *I* was supposed to be the psychologist. Shouldn't it be me dishing out the advice here?"

"If that were the case, you'd be stuck living in Pinegrove, bemoaning your sad state of loneliness, and not moving on with your life. That's why you have me. I give out awesome advice, like moving here, and the best part is, it's free."

This was why I loved Garreth. He didn't bullshit me and always told me like it was.

"I know, I know. You're right. I'll go to Black Light and have the best time. Who knows, maybe I'll meet the Dom of my dreams there."

He laughed. "That's the spirit. Now get some sleep, and call me when you get in town Thursday, okay?"

I saluted even though he couldn't see me. "Yes, Sir. Love ya. Tell that beautiful sub of yours I said hello too."

"Will do. Drive safe, and I'll see you when you get here. Night."

"Good night."

I disconnected the call and tossed my phone on the coffee table before finishing off my wine. My eyes scanned my living room and all the boxes stacked against the wall. I was going to miss my house, but I truly was excited to see what D.C., and Black Light, had to offer. I rinsed out my glass and headed to the bathroom to get ready for bed. Once in my sleep tank, I crawled under the covers, all the while knowing I'd never get to sleep. I'd been hoping the wine would help, but I was too wound up thinking about what the future held.

While I lay there, my mind drifted to the letter I received today. Of course Garreth knew about them. As did another Dom friend, Connor, who owned a security firm. He recommended I take them to the police, which I did. Unfortunately, they told me that since they weren't threatening in nature, merely a tad creepy, there wasn't much that could be done. I didn't know who'd written them so I couldn't get a restraining order. It was purely a wait and see if something happens and go from there scenario.

There was something I'd noticed in the last few months about them though that I don't think even Connor noticed. The 'voice' of the notes had changed slightly, right around the time Vince and I broke up. Whereas when they first began, they were almost child-like in their ardor. But these last few were more... I don't know, educated I guess. And much more graphic. It was so subtle though, I don't think anyone would notice if they weren't really studying them. But that's what I did. I studied the human mind. Which meant I analyzed each letter, trying to discover something about its author.

What type of person was sending them to me? And why me? Why did he — which wasn't an absolute that the author was a male, but I was pretty positive it wasn't a woman — why did he become so fixated on me? At first, I wondered if it was one of my patients, but I dismissed the thought. Chances were great it was someone I knew though. Regardless, I was glad to be leaving town.

When Garreth suggested moving to D.C., I practically jumped at the chance. Especially when he mentioned Black Light. I loved my local club, but I'd never developed a real connection with any of the Doms there, not even Vince. *Was there something fundamentally wrong with me?* I shook off the self-damaging thought.

I hadn't told anyone besides close friends where I was moving, which made me feel a little safer. I shivered a little at the sense of dread that suddenly crawled across the back of my neck, sending a chill through me. Ignoring the sensation, I flopped over onto my side and adjusted my pillow before closing my eyes, hoping sleep would come for me.

CHAPTER 2

oseph

With a weary sigh, my eyes scanned the room, stopping every few moments to take in a scene being played out. A lusciously curved sub was splayed out on a spanking bench, her juicy ass lightly pink from the love taps a Dom was using to warm her up. His barely-there handprint was quickly fading. Another sub was bound to the St. Andrew's cross, berry-red nipples tightly clamped and a look of drowsy ecstasy on her face that clearly showed how far into sub-space she was reaching. Yet, even being surrounded by dark and decadent pleasures, I was restless.

With another pass around the place, my gaze landed on my best friend striding toward me. Nat looked pissed. Which wasn't surprising. Lately, that seemed to be his primary emotion. Even more so than usual. He'd always been slightly volatile, but over the past six months, he'd become increasingly so. Enough that it was affecting our work. He reached the bar where I stood and dropped into the stool next to me without a greeting, merely a signal to the bartender. Klara made her way over.

"You seem overly chipper tonight."

Nathaniel's jaw clenched to hold back whatever bitter retort he'd been about to make at her sarcastic observation. It didn't matter that she was the Dungeon Master of Black Light's sub, Klara ran a tight ship and you didn't piss her off.

"Just a rough day," he bit out instead, while pulling a card out of his wallet and handing it to her. "I'll take a shot of Patron."

She produced a small wand and flipped the switch causing a bright purple light to glow and emanate from it. After waving it over Nat's card and keying his member number into her computer to keep track of his tab, she sent him another assessing glare before pivoting to fulfill his order. Finally, he turned to me.

"Rough day, huh?" I lounged back against the bar on my elbows.

His lip curled in a snarl while he rubbed his forehead as though warding off a headache. "You know it was. And thanks for sticking around after I got called into the Assistant Director's office, dickhead."

"What did you expect me to do? Your attitude is what got your ass in trouble. I know you're frustrated, but man, you can't keep running off at the mouth. You're gonna get yourself suspended, or worse, if you can't fix your shit. I tolerate it because you're my best friend. The higher ups we report to aren't going to."

"Damn it, Joseph, you don't think I know that?" He spun around in the bar stool and stood to mimic my pose, his gaze unfocused on everything in front of him. Not even the sharp cry of ecstasy coming from the raised platform not far from where we stood could drag his attention from the explosive emotions he kept restrained. "These last two cases have just gotten me off my game. The fucking 'Casanova' case has gone completely cold over the last six months, and the Russian is presumed dead. Yet we still have five dead women at the hands of that piece of shit serial killer and hundreds more missing, presumably as part of this goddamn sex trafficking ring. How am I supposed to react?"

I smacked his arm to get his attention back to me. "Definitely not by telling the Assistant Director he has his head so far up his boss' vagina that he wouldn't know how to solve a case if it was handed to him."

Nathaniel smirked a little. "I can't help it if it's true."

I only shook my head. "Regardless, the fact is, you need to keep that shit to yourself."

His expression dropped again and this time he scanned the room as if searching for someone. "I'm also feeling, I don't know, on edge I guess. Like something is supposed to happen, but I can't figure out what. There's this tingle at the base of my neck, a shift in the atmosphere somewhere signaling that whatever is coming, it's big."

Over the last five years working together, I'd learned not to ignore Nat's instincts. If he said something big was coming, I'd better brace myself.

"One shot of Patron. No salt. No lime."

Nathaniel turned back toward the bar, grabbed the shot glass, tipped a salute to Klara, and threw it down the hatch. With nary a shudder at the straight liquor no doubt burning a path down his throat, he set the glass on the bar top.

"My thanks, Klara."

She gave a small smile and snatched up the empty glass before disappearing down to the other end of the bar.

"You better watch it. Next thing you know, Spencer will be riding your ass about showing up here and irritating his woman."

"Klara secretly likes me, even if she busts my balls on occasion."

I ignored his comment and brought the conversation back to what was really bothering me. "I'm feeling the same way you are. The restlessness. The frustration. Everything's getting to me, and

I'm barely keeping things under control. Especially after Elizabeth."

Nathaniel's lip curled in disgust and his dark eyes blackened with loathing. "That bitch almost destroyed us. Spencer is lucky he revoked her membership. I wouldn't have been responsible for my actions."

Five months ago, Nat and I discovered the sub we'd been in a relationship with decided she wasn't interested in a ménage. In reality, she was a viper we'd unknowingly let into our bed. Looking back, I couldn't believe how dumb we'd been to let her try and play us against each other the way she had. Thankfully, we'd figured it out before she ravaged our friendship. I didn't blame him for his anger. I felt it too. Mine was just slower to simmer, while his was fiery and burned deep.

"Maybe we're both experiencing this agitation because we haven't had a woman in a while. We've come to Black Light every weekend for the last four months, and every time we've left alone and frustrated. At least I have. I'm ready to settle down, Nat. Start a family."

He let out a heavy sigh. "How do you think I feel? I'm closer to forty than thirty. I never thought I'd be saying this, but I want kids just as much as you do, Joseph. You were the one who kept telling me something didn't feel right with Elizabeth, that there wouldn't be any doubts if she was the one, but my stubborn ass didn't listen."

I'd just opened my mouth to respond when all the air was sucked out of me like a vacuum. Moving across the room was an angel in white. My vision tunneled to include only her. Toffee colored hair was bound on top of her head, a few tendrils cascading down to brush her cream colored shoulders. Even from this distance, I knew the top of her head would barely reach my chest. The large, tortoise shell glasses encompassed half her face, her eyes big and bright behind them. I was dying to see what color they were. Every inch of her body was flawless from the perfectly sized breasts to the dipped-in waist to the flared-out hips my fingers itched to grip.

Unconsciously, I took a step forward, but the hand on my arm stayed my movement. I jerked away and growled at the touch, ready to lash out at whomever was stopping me from meeting this woman.

"Earth to Joseph. What the hell, man?"

I shook my head at Nat's voice and the tunnel vision cleared, bringing the whole floor of Black Light back into focus. Still, my eyes never left her.

"We need to go meet her." My voice came out on a whisper.

"Who?" he asked in confusion.

I nodded in the direction the angel walked. "Her."

I sensed Nat move closer to me and when he drew in a hissed breath, I knew he'd spotted her too.

My eyes tracked her movement. Fate had brought her here tonight. Maybe she was the one we'd been looking for. Maybe not. Either way, I certainly intended to find out.

CHAPTER 3

$\mathcal{M}$adeline

WHEN THE CAB PULLED UP IN FRONT OF A STOREFRONT WITH A bright hand-painted sign saying *PSYCHIC* in bold purple lettering, I was confused. Where was this high-class club Garreth had talked up? He helped Hadlee out, then me, and my gaze darted up and down the street looking for something more. The bell above the door of the shop jingled when he opened it.

"Ladies." He gestured inside and I entered the store with him following on my heels. My eyes scanned the dimly lit shop, my nose twitching at the clash of scents filtering through the room. My feet were moving me forward, trying to figure out where the hell we were going when I almost ran into Hadlee.

"Hello, Luís."

I peeked over her shoulder, trying to see the person Garreth was greeting. It was then I spotted the Latino man sitting guard on an uncomfortable looking chair, half-hidden behind a curtain at the back of the shop. He smiled, lighting up his entire face and making the horrific looking scar running down the side of his face soften. He rose to greet us. The two men shook hands and he gave a respectful nod to Hadlee and me.

"Evening Garreth. Ladies. Be sure to have your membership card ready for Danny. You know how he is. Have a good night."

He turned and opened a door I only now noticed behind him. Like a lamb being led to slaughter, I continued following my escorts and shivered inside the cold, but well-lit, tunnel. My excitement was growing at the cloak and dagger type entrance we appeared to be making into Black Light. It all reeked of mystery and intrigue with all the dark halls and mysterious men guarding locked doors. Even though I remained confused, I was more eager to see where this was going. When we stopped at the next door, Garreth turned to us, but directed his comments to me.

"I know you don't need to be reminded, but I'm going to anyway. There will be some extremely prominent men and women inside here. People whose privacy is of the utmost importance. Parrish, I know you haven't been here long enough to recognize the majority of them, but confidentiality is a must. There are DMs available around the entire club if you need anything. There is also a two-drink limit that is strictly enforced. You'll have to put all your electronic devices in a locker. If you're ready to go before we are, you only need to say the word and we'll get out of here. In the meantime, let go of your shit and have fun."

Childishly, I stuck my tongue out at him, which only made Garreth shake his head and Hadlee chuckle.

"You're lucky you're not his sub. My ass would be on fire if I tried that move with him."

He reached for her hand and kissed her knuckles. "You know you love my punishments."

With that, he turned around and opened the door. Instantly the base of the tunnel was flooded with an iridescent purplish light that made everything glow. He gestured us through and when we turned a short corner, there stood a muscular man behind a security desk.

"Danny."

Muscular man smiled and looked less intimidating. "Garreth. Miss Hadlee." He lifted his chin in my direction. "A guest?"

"This is my best friend, Parrish."

Politely, I reached out to shake his hand. "You can call me Madeline."

Danny stared at my outstretched arm before placing his warm hand in mind. "Enjoy your evening, miss."

A glass window suddenly slid open and a woman spoke to us. "Good evening, Garreth."

"Maureen." He nodded in greeting while holding up his arm.

She swept a small wand emitting a purplish glowing light over his inner wrist. My forehead crinkled in puzzlement and then my eyes widened in awe at a brief glimpse of a barcode and number suddenly appearing on his flesh. *Holy hell, what kind of place was this?* I was actually impressed. Even my local, exclusive club back in North Carolina wasn't this high-tech and secure. Garreth hadn't told me much about the club, but it made me wonder what kind of people opened it that required this much security to get in.

Hadlee must have sensed my awe, because she squeezed my hand and whispered in my ear. "I'm glad you decided to come with us. I know you've been struggling lately, but I have no doubt you're going to have a great evening."

I smiled back at her, happy my best friend had found someone to love who was perfect for him.

"I'm sure I will." My response lacked confidence.

We were interrupted from further conversation when Garreth handed me a clipboard and the woman in the window rattled off instructions. "Read over these, initial each page, and sign the last one. All of your personal belongings, including all electronic devices, will need to go into a locker before you're allowed entry.

If you need any assistance, please don't hesitate to find a dungeon monitor."

I tuned out most of what she'd been saying as I scanned the NDA in front of me. From what I could tell, it was a typical agreement. I scribbled my initials on each page before signing it and handing it back to her.

Garreth pulled his wallet out and handed over cash.

"You don't need to pay my way. I've got it."

His only response was to shoot me a glare and my mouth snapped shut, even as I scowled right back.

"Left hand, please."

I startled at the forgotten woman's command. Knowing there was no point in arguing with Garreth right now, I stuck my arm out and she turned it over before stamping the inside of my wrist. I couldn't see what she'd stamped on me, but I could feel the coldness of the wet ink before it dissipated as it dried. We headed over to the wall of lockers and I stashed my purse with phone inside the designated metal compartment.

"You ready?" Hadlee asked.

I looked over at her and almost laughed as she stood there giddy and almost bouncing with energy. "As I'll ever be."

We left the locker room and my breath caught at the club in front of me. Not even the club back in Pinegrove prepared me for the debauchery going on at Black Light. Suddenly, my whole body became lighter. It was like I'd come home. In wide-eyed wonder I wandered my way through the club forgetting entirely about Garreth and Hadlee. I stopped at one of the raised platforms that seemed to be spread randomly around the room to observe a scene going on. I shivered with arousal while I watched a Dom wield one of my favorite implements, the Wartenberg wheel. My nipples pebbled as I imagined the prickly points running over my skin.

My eyes continued to wander the room, and I struggled to take everything in. All my senses were firing, and I was feeling that endorphin-infused high. There was a frosted glass window like you'd see at the doctor's office. That must be the medical/doctor play area Garreth had told me about.

I found myself flitting across the entire floor absorbing the sights, sounds, and smells of Black Light. There was nothing like hearing cries of ecstasy mixed with searing pain. The smell of sex was strong and teased my nose with the hope of what might come from the night. The musky scent had my core throbbing with a need unlike any I remember ever experiencing before. My body was ready to play. The problem was finding a likeminded partner.

I startled when a deep voice sounded far closer to my ear than I expected.

"I really hope you're not looking for your Dom... unless of course it's me you're looking for."

I inhaled a sharp gasp when I laid eyes on the man who'd spoken. The biggest and brightest blue orbs stared back at me, surrounded by sculpted cheekbones and a jaw that seemed to be chiseled from stone with a small patch of hair covering about an inch of the tip of his chin.

"And me."

My head whipped to my other side where another breathtaking man stood so close I could feel the heat emanating off his trim, muscular body. His essence was in complete contrast to the almost light aura coming from his younger counterpart. This man was all dark. From his hair to the burning fire in his deep brown eyes. There was an intensity that made me want to purr at his feet.

"Cat got your tongue, love?"

My eyes jerked back up to meet mocha-colored eyes that I thought held a hint of humor, but I couldn't be sure because his expression gave none of his emotions away. They both shifted positions until they stood directly in front of me and I was thankful I wouldn't get whiplash jerking my head back and forth between them. Silence continued until I realized his question wasn't rhetorical.

"No, I'm perfectly capable of speech." I could taste the bitterness of the almost-lie on my tongue. They had no idea the effort it had taken me to form those six words. It was the first time in a long time I'd been struck dumb by a Dom. Let alone two of them.

"Perhaps you'd tell us your name then?" Blue eyes spoke this time.

I batted my eyelashes in an unpracticed move of flirtation. It felt awkward and unnatural so I had no idea why I'd even tried, but some insane part of my brain was leading things at the moment.

"Perhaps."

A deep growl came from the dark beast with brown eyes. "Coyness doesn't become you."

I blinked at the assessment, because he was one hundred percent correct. I didn't have a coy bone in my body, and the fake emotion was clearly obvious. My eyes lowered in deference.

"You're right. I apologize. My name is Madeline."

A finger under my chin tilted my head up and I stared into heated dark eyes. "That's better. I'm Nathaniel and this is Joseph. However, tonight you can call us Master."

CHAPTER 4

 oseph

VIOLET. HER EYES WERE THE MOST STUNNING SHADE OF VIOLET. I could almost get lost in them. I was also curious to see how she responded to Nat. He was being aggressively forward, but between the two of us he enjoyed the slightly darker elements of our lifestyle — my penchant for breath play not withstanding. If she couldn't handle what he dished out, no matter how disappointed I ended up, it was best to find out now.

Madeline's eyes darkened at Nat's command and her pupils dilated in arousal. I swore she let out a soft sigh of content. I waited with bated breath, wondering how she'd respond to the simple, but forceful, instruction. I could sense her indecision, and wasn't sure if it was Nat's presumptive nature or something else holding her back. Nat's expression turned predatory when she blinked those gorgeous orbs and made her decision with a softly uttered, "Yes, Master."

I leaned down and murmured into her ear. "You won't regret this, Madeline. We'll take extremely good care of you."

She looked us over and her lips turned up. "I'm looking forward to it. Master." She tacked on the honorific at the end.

"Is there anyone you need to check in with?" Nat questioned.

The few tendrils of hair fluttered back and forth when she shook her head. "My friends are here, but they encouraged me to play."

"Good," he nodded. "Why don't we all get to know each other a little better first."

We crooked our arms and waited to see if she'd accept our escort. I let out a breath of relief when, after only a slight hesitation, Madeline threaded her hands through our waiting arms. Nat and I both kept some distance from her. No need to crowd her and scare her off before we even got a chance to talk— and hopefully play afterward. We led her to a small table with a front row seat to a wax play scene playing out on the raised dais in front of us. Normally, I'd take the opportunity to observe one of my favorite kinks, but our violet-eyed angel had my full and complete attention. My eyebrows raised when Nat played the gentleman and pulled out Madeline's seat. As she sat, he pushed the chair in and his hand swept across the back of her neck when he moved to his own chair. I hid my smile when a faint flush crossed her cheeks at his touch. It would seem the little sub was affected by our presence.

Once all three of us were seated, I discovered I was too far away from the beautiful woman at my left. Catching Nat's gaze, I eyed the distance between our seats. We'd been a team long enough that he read my thoughts and practically in unison, we slid our chairs closer to Madeline. Close enough that there was an intimacy to our conversation without her feeling like she was closed in without a way to escape.

"Just so you know, there are DMs here to make sure all play is safe, sane, and consensual," I reassured her.

She smiled and I couldn't help but respond in kind. "My best friend is actually a dungeon monitor here. Tonight's his night off though."

Well, that was a surprise. "Oh, and who might that be?"

"Garreth."

"We know him well. I'm curious though... why we haven't seen you here before tonight? He surely would have introduced you to the pleasures at Black Light."

Nat reached out and traced his finger along the back of Madeline's hand resting on the table, his tone dropping an octave as he drew out the word 'pleasures.' She inhaled sharply and her eyes darkened with arousal, all while she shivered at his touch. It was so subtle I almost missed it, but I knew Nat hadn't since his nostrils flared like he was scenting prey. Curious about her reaction, I set my hand on her thigh, low and close to her knee. She shifted in her seat, and her muscles twitched, but she didn't move away. Instead, her flush deepened and moved down her chest. I wanted to follow its path. Were her nipples cherry red or brown like my favorite caramel? My mouth watered at the thought of finding out. I was picturing the perfect shade of red wax that would complement the color of her blush.

Madeline spoke up, interrupting my delicious thoughts. "I'm new to the city actually."

"You've never visited before?" Nat asked.

She shook her head. "I've been to D.C. several times, but it's been a couple years. Long before Black Light opened."

"What brought you here if you don't mind me asking?"

Pain flared in her eyes before she squashed it and shrugged. "Change of scenery, I guess."

Neither Nat nor I tolerated lies, and it was obvious her answer was an untruth. Or at least not the whole truth. She wasn't our sub, yet, so I let it pass. For now.

This time she volleyed back her own question. "Do you often share women?"

Nat guffawed with genuine amusement. It was the first time I'd seen him truly smile in longer than I could remember. Maybe a year or more.

"We always share a woman, pet."

That's when I moved my hand, sliding it slowly up her thigh, stopping only when I reached the hem of her dress. Any further than that required an okay from her, and I waited to receive it. When she didn't utter any protest, I continued my sensual advance. My finger made its way under fabric and Madeline's legs parted to give my hand more room. Her breathing grew shallow and her eyes darted back and forth between us. Nat added sensation by running his finger between hers, teasing the webbing between them and drawing on her palm.

"Do you have any reservations about being shared between two men, Madeline?" Physically she appeared to be saying yes, but I wanted verbal consent so there was no miscommunication between any of us.

"No." Her voice came out breathy.

In sync, Nat and I both stopped all movement. Instantly, she recognized her mistake and corrected herself. "I mean, no, Master."

"Tsk, tsk, pet. I believe that little lapse comes with a punishment."

She moaned under her breath as if in anticipation. Hmmm, interesting. It was time to move this show along. My cock was humming with need. I wanted to bury it deep inside this woman. To feel her from the inside out. Her pussy. Her mouth. Her ass. It didn't matter. In the end, we'd own every hole. My gut told me she was the one we'd been searching for and it wasn't usually wrong.

"I believe our sub here might enjoy our form of correction. What do you think, Nat?"

Nat winked at me and gave a short upward chin tilt. "I definitely agree with you. But why don't you check and see? I'd hate for us to be wrong."

With a flick of my wrist, my finger came in contact with smooth, wet pussy. I didn't think my cock could get any harder, but unexpectedly coming across bare skin instead of satin fabric made a liar out of me.

I chuckled. "Nat, our naughty little pet here isn't wearing any underwear. And she's sopping. There's no doubt a puddle of her sweet pussy juice beneath her. I bet she's going to taste delicious."

A deep masculine rumble was his response. I rubbed up and down her slick pussy slit, teasing the opening with the tip of my finger, but not penetrating further. Instead, my finger moved, increasing the contact on the upward swipe to graze her clit with each stroke. My gaze bore into hers as I confirmed what we both knew, even as her moan of pleasure confirmed it. "The thought of us punishing you turns you the fuck on, doesn't it? You're gushing just thinking about all the dirty, wicked, perverse things we're going to do to you."

Madeline's hips moved under the gentle coaxing of my finger as more wetness poured from her. She bit her lip, but another sound of ecstasy still escaped. "Yes, Master."

Letting the anticipation build, I kept stroking her, teasing her clit — fast, then slow — as the smell of her arousal wafted around us. She squirmed in her chair, legs now fully splayed open, her juice practically pooling on the seat beneath her. Her eyes began to close behind her lenses, and I could see her muscles tensing in preparation for her orgasm. When I could tell she was on the precipice of tumbling over, I pulled my hand away at the same time Nat let go of her hand. Her expression shifted, her eyes popped open, and she blinked. Blinked again. Then her adorable mouth turned into a pout.

"Why did you stop? I was almost there."

I smiled wickedly. "Yes, I know. Let's just call that the prelude to your punishment. Now, we need to negotiate our scene before we go any further."

The few tendrils of hair around her face fluttered when she let out a small, annoyed huff of air. Nat and I both liked the challenge of a sub with just a bit of defiance in her. Not a complete brat, but enough spark to make it interesting.

"What are your hard limits? And do you have a safe word?"

I was curious about her response considering I knew Nat's kinks. Out of the corner of my eye, I watched his reaction.

Matter-of-factly, she ticked them off. "My hard limits include watersports and scat, humiliation, whipping, and anything that leaves permanent markings. Oh, no needles either."

"How do you feel about knife play?"

There was a devious twinkle in his eyes at her answers. I knew Nat would push her limits with his love of the knife. For him though, it wasn't about the cutting per se, although he certainly enjoyed seeing his shallow marks on a sub's skin. He also didn't bleed anyone unless they enjoyed it. It was the mind-fuck, the fear, that turned him on.

She took a moment to ponder her answer. "Honestly, I don't know. I've never experienced it before. Is blood involved? Because that would definitely be a hard limit."

Nat replied since this was his area of expertise. "For me, it's not about the blood. It's the rush of the mindfuck. It's a heady feeling knowing that my sub trusts me enough to not damage her body. On occasion, I like to leave some scratches, a reminder, but they're shallow and I don't fully break the skin. Of course, there is definitely a tremendous amount of trust involved, because sometimes things happen. But I always take every safety precaution before engaging in any play, especially with someone inexperienced in it. If it's something you'd like to try sometime, I'm more than willing to oblige."

I was glad she took her time, weighing the idea instead of immediately shooting it down. The power of the knife really was an integral part of him. Nat would accept her limits though.

"Let's table that one for another time. For now, I'm going to say it's a hard limit with the option to change my mind."

"Understood. I hope to change your mind soon," he added with a cheeky grin.

"I hope you do, too," Madeline replied just as cheekily.

"Well, now that we've learned your hard limits, we should also share ours. We draw the line at electrical play and age play. Neither are our special kind of kink."

"So you won't spank me and make me call you Daddy then, huh?" She smirked, a sparkle shining from behind her glasses.

Nat slowly rose from his seat, causing Madeline to tilt her head way back to track his movements. She shifted nervously in her seat, swallowing hard, most likely realizing she'd awakened the beast inside him. He took one step forward and threaded his fingers through her hair, fisting the strands and gently, but firmly, pulling her up and out of her chair. He leaned down and rasped his stubble across her cheek and jaw before whispering in her ear.

"There will most definitely be spanking involved, pet. My hand is already twitching with the need to redden that ass of yours. You're spunky and full of fire and I like it. But I think it's time now for that punishment you earned."

I could see her tremble from the hot breath blowing against her as he continued.

"Along with a new one it looks like we'll be adding to it. Just so you don't forget it's Master, not Daddy. Now, be a good submissive and tell us your safe word." He nipped her ear, emphasizing the command behind his directive and she sagged against him, her hands clutching his biceps as though to hold herself up. Nat braced his palm around her hip to help keep her steady.

Her eyes were heavy-lidded with arousal and it took her a moment to get her bearings. Once she had, she wobbled a bit as though weak in the knee. I stood and moved behind her, effectively caging her between us as I traced my finger down her arm, causing her to shiver.

On a shaky breath, she exhaled her answer. "Dragonfly."

"Good girl. Now, are you ready to accept your punishment, Madeline?"

"Yes, Master."

CHAPTER 5

$\mathcal{M}$adeline

I COULDN'T REMEMBER BEING THIS TURNED ON IN MY LIFE, AND neither of them had really even touched me. But God did I want them to. There was this edge, sharp and honed, to Nathaniel that was awakening something inside me. It was unlike anything I'd ever felt before. I didn't tend to mentally pick apart the Doms I scened with, but there was a dark depravity I sensed emanating from him that my clinician brain couldn't help but want to analyze. I had a feeling I'd drown in the darkness with him. And revel in it.

Joseph was different. He was the buoy. The one that would keep us all afloat. I don't know how I knew this after being in their presence for such a short time, but I did. I also knew I didn't plan on questioning it. I wanted to be punished by them, to test my limits, and my body quivered in anticipation.

Nathaniel clasped my hand in his and led me to the raised platform nearest us. There was a spanking bench at its center.

Our footsteps clicked on the wooden planking making up the floor. Joseph stepped into my line of sight, but remained on the carpeted area surrounding us.

"Glasses, please." Nathaniel held his hand out and I placed them in his palm. My skin prickled as Joseph stayed where he was, his eyes tracking a path up and down the length of my body. His eyes glowed with appreciation. Footsteps sounded behind me and then I felt my dress lifted. Cool air brushed across my thighs, my ass, my back, and my breasts before the dress briefly covered my face and then it was finally pulled over my head. I stood proudly naked, my breasts full and heavy with need. Joseph's blue eyes had deepened in color so they now resembled the ocean water during a vicious storm. Strong hands cupped my breasts, squeezing and caressing them, sending sweet pleasure spiraling through my core.

"Can you sense the people watching us? Joseph watching us? Their eyes absorbing the sight of these perfect tits." He squeezed them again, pinching at my nipples, my breath hitching at the exquisite sensation. His hand skimmed down my stomach and cupped my pussy, his fingers teasing my entrance. "This wet, needy cunt. Watching, waiting, for me to do this." He crooked a finger and pushed it gently, slowly inside me before sliding it almost completely out. When he moved again, I moaned at the fuller sensation as he added another finger. My knees trembled and I wasn't sure how much longer they would hold me.

"Are you ready for your punishment now, pet?"

I opened eyes I hadn't realized I'd close to see Joseph stepping onto the wooden flooring now standing directly on the other side of the bench, his pants tented with an impressive looking erection. "Yes, Master."

"Position yourself properly then." Nathaniel punctuated his command with a stinging swat to my bottom cheeks.

Stepping up to the spanking bench, I settled my spread knees onto the padded leg pieces. I sucked in a breath as the cool leather touched my skin causing my bare belly to clench, and a shiver raced over me bringing goosebumps to my arms. I knew the cold wouldn't last long though. I bowed my head while I waited for whatever my Masters had planned.

"Eyes up, Madeline."

I raised my head, and my gaze followed Joseph's hands as he slowly lowered the zipper on his pants revealing smooth skin. He pulled out his cock and like Pavlov's dog, my mouth started to water. I wanted to wrap my lips around its smooth, rounded head and lap up the salty pre-cum I could see glistening from its tip.

"Nat, I think our sub here likes what she sees. What do you think?"

From behind me came the gruff response. "Let's find out."

Calloused fingers gripped my ass cheeks and spread me open wide, exposing everything to his view. A warm, wet tongue swiped up my lower lips, lapping at the juices flowing from my wet pussy and I cried out at the sensation.

"You're right. She fucking loves it."

"Good, because you're going to suck it and drink down every drop I give you. I'm not going to be gentle. I'm going to fuck your mouth hard and you're going to take every inch I give you. Understand?"

I didn't know how I was going to take him all, but I knew he wasn't going to give me any leeway. There was only one answer I could give. "Yes, Master."

"Nat, warm her ass up."

"With pleasure," came his rumbled reply.

Smack. My ass stung with the strike and a heat began to spread. I knew that this was just the beginning. My real punishment would come before I knew it. Smack. Nathaniel's bare hand came down again almost in the same spot. The next few came in rapid succession. I couldn't help but squeak and jump with each one. My ass was tingling and burning.

I was so focused on when and where the next strike might come, I missed Joseph's movement until he pulled my hair — that had long started falling out of the hair tie holding it up — forcing my head back. I gasped and bit my bottom lip in ecstasy as I stared at the delectable cockhead staring directly at me. It was even more delicious up close, leaking pre-cum, and the long vein running its length was almost daring me to trace it with my tongue.

"Open," came the guttural command.

When my mouth widened, Joseph slid his cock inside, but not quite far enough to hit the back of my throat. Yet. He'd already warned me it was coming. He pulled back and just when he was almost all the way out, he thrust forward again, this time going further. Back and forth he pushed and pulled, his grip on my hair tightening inside his fist with each inward motion of his cock. The piston motion sped up and with each thrust he pushed further inside until, with one sharp jerk, he went so deep my gag reflex activated and I coughed and choked. My eyes watered and I was sure my mascara was running down my cheeks.

He pulled back and let me take a deep inhale. This time, he went slower and when he reached the back of my throat, I swallowed and relaxed, letting him slip a little further back. Spit pooled in my mouth and leaked out the sides as he held immobile. Yet, I still hadn't taken his entire length. My eyes watered even more and when I didn't think I could take anymore, he pulled out, a thread of saliva keeping us connected before it snapped.

"That was beautiful, pet. You're just about ready to take it all. But poor Nathaniel back there, he's missing out. I think he needs some place to put his cock as well. What do you think?"

"Please." My pussy begged to be filled.

A sharp smack on my already sore ass cheek made me cry out.

"Naughty sub. I think you forgot the magic word. You must not want this pretty pink cunt filled after all." Nathaniel taunted me by rubbing his thickness between my pussy lips, teasing the opening but not entering. Even through the condom I hadn't noticed he'd slipped on, he was so hot and thick I was having a hard time concentrating on what I'd done wrong, when another spank had me remembering quickly.

"Please, Master, fill my pussy," I begged.

"What do you think, Nathaniel? Did our pretty sub ask nicely enough?" Joseph taunted, denying the pleasure awaiting me.

"I think we should take pity on her this one time. She's sweet, pink, and soft. And she's begging us." I almost sighed in relief at Nathaniel's response.

Yes, please.

Joseph, on the other hand, never mentioned he was a sadist. "I don't know if she's been punished well enough for her multiple infractions. She has earned them. Maybe you need to warm her ass up a little more. Besides, the extra pinch of pain will make her pleasure that much sweeter."

I whimpered in frustration. My pussy clenched on emptiness.

"Perhaps a little orgasm denial will help her remember who this pussy belongs to for the evening."

I let out another whimper. They were going to kill me.

Nathaniel chuckled deviously, the deep tone settling low in my belly. "I think that's a suitable punishment. Mostly because it means we can prolong our play."

He moved over me, his cock sliding through my slit and butting up against my clit, laying his front against my back as he leaned down to nip my shoulder, caging me between his arms. "Whose pussy is this?" He punctuated his question with a short thrust.

I pressed back against him, trying to deepen our contact, but Nathaniel wasn't having any of it. He swatted my hip, leaving a sting in his wake.

"If you don't stay still, we'll tie you to this bench and add another punishment to your tally. Right now, you're only at two. Are you sure you want to aim for three?"

"I'm sorry, Master."

"What a pretty apology. I think you've earned a small reward for that. But first, answer the question. Whose pussy is this?"

"Yours Master."

In response, Nathaniel moved off me. His fingers gripped my hips and his thumbs separated my cheeks. I expected to feel his wet tongue against my pussy again. I squeaked when instead he flicked the tip of it against my anus before tracing the rim of it. He spread my cheeks wider, opening me even further to his exploration. He lapped at my asshole, the bundle of nerves tingling with each swipe of his tongue. His touch deepened when he pushed it inside tasting and exploring every inch of me.

The tingling spread, and the added sensation of a thumb dipping just inside my sopping wet pussy, had me gasping for breath. I was chasing an orgasm I knew wasn't going to come, but I was helpless to resist its pull. The tension was building and just when it was about to explode, Nathaniel pulled away. A sharp smack to my cheek, startling me, pushed it even further away. I cried out in disappointment. Joseph, who was still clutching my hair in his fist, released his hold and smoothed back my hair, almost petting me as if to soften the blow.

"You're doing beautifully. Take this spanking like a good sub and you'll feel pleasure like never before. Can you do that for us?" Joseph's voice was gentle and calming and it made me want to please them all the more.

"Yes, Master."

"Good girl," he praised me. "Nat, go ahead."

Before his words faded, my ass was on fire. Blow after blow rained down on me, the sharp pain of each strike burning through me. I flinched with each swat, no longer able to hold back my tears as Nathaniel continued his relentless punishment. I lost count of how many he delivered. I only knew the pain was morphing, shifting into an almost numb sensation that was swiftly spreading through me. Just as quickly as my punishment began, it stopped. My head was buzzing and a warm feeling blanketed me.

"Now comes the pleasure."

I barely registered the words spoken in my ear when I was rocked forward with a single thrust of Nathaniel's cock as he buried himself to the hilt inside me sliding easily through the wetness. The fullness of his cock took my breath away, and I cried out at the abrasion against my battered ass. My entire body felt alive with a combination of pain and pleasure. Sparks singed my insides, but I wanted to feel the burn. It was invigorating.

I couldn't help but push back against him when he pulled almost out and then thrust even harder back in. He began a slow and steady rhythm, one that was driving me mad. I needed the friction of his movement to speed up and send me over the edge, but I knew that he and Joseph would decide when it was time. I was the puppet dancing on their strings, and they were the Masters controlling the tempo. The wait would be worth it though, so I continued to dance.

"Are you ready, pet?" My vision homed in on Joseph who'd been patiently waiting for this moment. My final punishment to complement the pleasure Nathaniel was giving me. One I was going to thoroughly enjoy. The saliva had already begun to pool in my mouth at the thought of his taste inside again. It was going to be difficult to not disappoint him with my concentration divided between Nathaniel's cock in my pussy and swallowing everything Joseph was about to give me, but I was going to do my damnedest. I wanted to give this to them. To be at their mercy. To be used utterly and completely by them both.

"I'm more than ready, Master." My voice trembled on the honorific as Nathaniel pinched my clit even as his movements ceased. Every part of me was on fire. My body was covered in a sheen of sweat, and the tiny hairs framing my face stuck to my skin.

Joseph beamed in pride at my confident response. It was true. I wanted this. Needed it. Relished in it. I was meant to meet these men here tonight. Everything about them spoke to a deviant side of me I never knew existed until now. They harnessed it and led it by its leash.

"Open," Joseph once again commanded. Without hesitation, my mouth widened and he slid his length inside. Then, in opposing tandem, they began to move. First, Joseph thrust inside the cavern of my mouth. When he pulled back, Nathaniel pushed deeper inside my wet heat. Like two people who knew each other well, their timing was perfect. Neither one rushed the other. They were entirely in sync.

"It's time to fly, pet." Without giving me time to process Joseph's words, it began. Nathaniel's thrusts shortened while Joseph's grew deeper. He pushed further into my mouth until at long last, my nose brushed up against his stomach. Pulling out enough for me to gulp in a large breath of air, he was quickly back down my throat completely, his shallow thrusting growing more aggressive. Saliva dripped out the corners of my mouth and suddenly Joseph stiffened and my throat moved of its own accord, swallowing every ounce he gave me. He pulled out and I gasped in a lungful of air at the same time Nathaniel thrust deeper inside me with one smooth motion.

On my next breath, Nathaniel pinched my clit and the orgasm that had been lying in wait rushed forth and coursed through me. I screamed out my release, echoing Nathaniel's roar of pleasure. I lay there gasping, panting for breath, my sweat-covered skin growing cold in the cool air of the club. My limbs were like noodles and I wasn't sure I wanted to move even if I could. I was so sleepy and content... and happy. An emotion I hadn't completely been in ages. I wanted to bask in it. In that moment, the connection I felt with these two men was tangible, visceral. It was on a whole other plane. I whimpered in disappointment when Nathaniel began to pull out, and I clenched my pussy trying to pull him back in.

I felt myself being moved from the bench and I clutched tightly to the man who held me. I recognized Joseph's voice in my ear.

"You were absolutely stunning, pet. Breathtaking. I knew you were perfect for us the second I saw you. I just knew it." I didn't try to decipher his words. Instead, I basked in them. My eyes fluttered open and my fuzzy brain tried to focus on where I was. I didn't immediately see Nathaniel and my heart ached. Where was he?

Joseph sat on a couch and pulled me onto his lap. A warm blanket was draped over me and then a water bottle clasped in a large hand appeared in front of me.

"Drink for me."

I relaxed when I saw it was Nathaniel holding the bottle to my mouth, tipping it gently when I opened, letting the cool liquid slowly pour between my parched lips. When I was finished, he set the bottle aside and knelt beside us, his hand reaching out to grasp mine. His touch was soothing as his thumb rubbed gently across my knuckles. I needed this physical connection with him as well. I clutched his hand tightly, not wanting him to let go. Our eyes remained on each other and our breathing soon matched. Peace flowed through me.

CHAPTER 6

$\mathcal{N}$athaniel

PROVIDING AFTERCARE TO A SUB HAD TO BE ONE OF THE MOST fulfilling aspects of being a Dom. To know that I'm providing comfort after a scene was so gratifying. With Madeline, it was even more so. The utter trust she'd offered both Joseph and me during the scene and after made this entire evening worth it. I glance up and saw his eyes were transfixed on Madeline. When he sensed my stare, he looked down at me and unspoken words shifted between us.

Neither of us had felt this instant connection with a sub before. Joseph always claimed he believed in love at first sight. I never knew if he was serious or not. However, I definitely acknowledged the fact that there was something about this woman that drew me to her. A warmth. Whatever it was, I wanted more of it. I wanted to get to know her, not just here at Black Light, but outside, in the real world. I wanted to hear her laugh. To hold her in my arms. I wanted people to know she was with us, however temporary. It wasn't logical, but the desire was undeniable.

I brushed back the dried hair from her face and cupped her cheek, needing the physical connection with her as I was coming to the realization that this was worth exploring further. She nuzzled my palm, her expression still a little drowsy.

"How are you feeling, pet?" I asked softly.

Madeline shook off her sleepiness and grinned. "Absolutely wonderful, Master. Thank you."

"Good. If you're ready, I want to head to the bar. You need food."

I held out my hand and pulled her off Joseph's lap when she placed hers in mine. Joseph handed me her dress, and I helped her back into it. Next came her glasses and, with a gentleness I'd long forgotten I possessed, I replaced them on her face. She blinked her wide violet eyes up at me. With Joseph on her other side, I led her over to a table in front of the bar, pulling out her chair and helping her get settled in it. We took our seats directly on either side of her, and I motioned for a server. Once she took our order, she quickly left, leaving the three of us alone.

In unison, Joseph and I reached out and clasped each of her hands in one of ours. Her skin was silky smooth. I could touch her forever and never get tired of it. There were so many things I wanted to ask her, but I was never good at that kind of thing. Thankfully, Joseph knew me well enough and started up the conversation I wanted to.

"I know this is a little backwards, considering how our night has progressed, but we'd love to get to know you a little better. I'll start. I'm Joseph Crocker. I've been a Dom for ten years, since shortly after I graduated from Columbia. My folks are still married and live in Upstate New York. I have two brothers and a sister, all older, and a slew of nieces and nephews. I'm a huge fan of college basketball and Nat and I have worked together at the FBI for the last five years."

"Wow, the FBI huh? And you guys are partners?"

Joseph shook his head. "There aren't really such things as 'partners' in the FBI. We're actually part of the same team, and more often than not, we're sent out into the field together, but that's mostly because I'm the only one who tolerates this jackass."

He chin-tilted in my direction. A single finger was my response. Madeline's gaze ping-ponged between us like she wasn't sure how to take our banter.

"What about you?" Impatient as always, I prompted her to give us some info. I'd be happy learning anything.

"Madeline Parrish. I recently moved to D.C. from North Carolina where I was a practicing clinical psychologist for the past eight years. I've been sexually submissive for as long as I can remember, but I didn't really understand what it meant until my last year of under-grad. One of my girlfriends got me into the local dungeon, and the minute I walked in I felt like I was home."

She turned to me. I could sense that she understood I didn't care to talk about myself and when she didn't say anything, I appreciated that she didn't force me to talk before I was ready. She merely waited patiently. I wasn't big on talking. It was something I'd never excelled at. I was more of an action kind of guy and feelings weren't really my 'thing.'

I gruffly gave her a response. "Nathaniel Morgan. Not much to tell. I didn't know I was a Dom until I met Joseph. But the minute I recognized the need for control inside me, I fully embraced it and haven't looked back. Now, I'm done talking about myself. We want to see you again. Outside of here."

She looked between us, studying us both before responding. I held my breath waiting for the answer I hoped she'd give.

"I'd really like that."

Muscles I hadn't realized were tight loosened, and I exhaled in relief. I knew Joseph had been nervous about her response as well. There were times I envied his ability to fall so quickly for someone. He'd been in awe of her since the moment he'd seen her.

But I also knew he would be a little cautious with his feelings. We'd been burned before.

"Great. There's a concert upstairs at Runway this coming Friday. Then, after it's over, we can move down here. We'll pick you up at seven."

Her blinking eyes behind her glasses were the only sign of her surprise at Joseph's demand. She was going to have to get used to it. When it came to certain things, we didn't ask.

"Runway?" Her forehead crinkled adorably with confusion.

"It's the premier dance club in D.C.," Joseph explained. "Sits right on top of us. Both clubs are owned by Jaxson Davidson and Chase Cartwright. You didn't come into Black Light through the club?"

She shook her head. "No, we came through a psychic shop. You mean there's another entrance?"

"Oh yeah, there's one through Runway and one from the shop. Black Light is extremely exclusive and even more private and confidential. There are a lot of prominent people who are members here and secrecy is of the utmost importance."

Madeline seemed impressed. "I had no idea. I mean, Garreth had mentioned its exclusivity, but I didn't realize to what degree."

Wanting to get back on track, I brought the conversation back to our next date. My body tingled oddly with anxiousness. "So, Friday night. Seven. We'll pick you up."

She released my hand to salute smartly. "Yes, Master."

"Oh, pet, I can't wait to tame that mouth of yours."

"If ever any beauty I did see, which I desired, and got,'twas but a dream of thee."
- John Donne, The Good-Morrow

My dearest Madeline,

I dreamed of you last night. You were standing on the shore of the lake, your unbound hair tangling around your face as the wind whipped it to and fro. Your hand shaded your eyes as you looked out over the water, watching the sun fall below the horizon. The yellows, oranges, pinks, and purples of the dusk-filled sky drew a smile to your beautiful lips. It was a smile that eclipsed even the disappearing sun. I wanted to take a picture of that smile, to capture it forever.

I waited in the distance, not wanting to disturb you. My patience was fairly tested though when you remained standing there, long after the sun disappeared and even as the moon glowed brightly above the water, illuminating the entire sky. Your only movement came when you wrapped your arms around yourself as you shivered in the cold night air. Just as I was about to call out to you, you turned and began walking toward me. You held your head high, the smile no longer visible, as you moved with grace across the sand, coming ever closer to me. I held my breath as you finally reached the place I stood. Hesitantly, as though you might disappear, I raised my hand to cup your cheek in my palm. Your skin was soft as silk beneath my fingertips.

My heart hitched in my throat though as tears filled your eyes. They spilled over and left a trail of moisture down your face. As I continued to stare at you, the tears changed. They turned from clear, to pink, to red, until soon, they were the deepest shade; the color of blood. Your mouth parted on a silent cry, but no sound escaped. Faster and faster your tears fell, with no end in sight.

Slowly, I unbuttoned your blouse, each tiny enclosure released to expose your glorious breasts to my view. I pushed the fabric back behind your shoulders, and I couldn't help but admire the vision of beauty in front of me, even as the blood-red tears dripped from your chin to dot *across your chest. You didn't even flinch. You only stood silent and unmoving.*

My vision homed in on a cluster of droplets. I cocked my head as I studied them, and it was then that I saw the shape that had formed. I smiled as I reached out and traced the design that had fallen with precision. Because you see, my dearest Madeline, your tears of blood had formed a heart. A heart that will soon belong to me.

Until we meet again.

CHAPTER 7

$\mathcal{N}$athaniel

"MORGAN, CROCKER, GET IN HERE. NOW."

I cursed under my breath at the command from the other room. Assistant Director Reynolds was still pissed off and punishing me for my comment last week. Knowing it was best to move my ass, I stood from behind my chipped particleboard desk, my raggedy chair squeaking with the release of my weight. I was two steps behind Joseph as he led the way to our boss' office. Once inside, we took our seats while we watched him pace and run his fingers through his hair. We waited in silence for him to finish whatever mental exercise he appeared to be engaged in. Finally, he stopped pacing and moved to perch on the edge of his desk, his arms crossed over his chest.

"I got a call from the P.D. over in Arlington. There's a woman there who received an anonymous letter from a 'secret admirer' she says. Normally, I wouldn't give a shit about some sad-ass woman getting a letter she thinks is from a crazy stalker, but from what the detective says, it sounds like this could be one of our little notes from Casanova. I need you guys to head over there and check it out. She's probably just someone in desperate need of the attention."

I bit my tongue from responding. Dick. This right here was why he sat his ass behind a desk and diddled himself. How he ever became the A.D., I'll never know. He probably sucked the right cock... or pussy. The fact remained, he was a douche. Joseph, the ever-cool-headed one of us, spoke up, probably because he knew I stood on the verge of blowing a gasket.

"Yes, sir. We'll be happy to head over and check things out. Hopefully, it's just a rejected lover making idle threats. We'll report back ASAP if it's something needing further investigation."

"See that you do." He nodded a dismissal, and we rose from our seats and exited the office without another word.

I held my terse comments until we got to our vehicle. "What a jackass." I slammed the door behind me in irritation.

Joseph slowly left the parking lot before responding. "That may be true, but sadly, we report to him. Which means, no matter how much he pisses us off, we have to toe the line, not nosedive over the edge of it."

I merely shot him an annoyed glance. Soon, we were pulling into the local precinct. We made our way up to the desk where a heavyset, completely disinterested beat cop sat behind scratched up plexiglass pecking away at an old desktop computer; one with a giant boxy monitor dating back to the nineties. His name badge read 'Hopkins.' Officer Hopkins didn't bother to look up when we stepped up to the window. That is, until I slapped my ID against it. His bored drawl had my teeth clenching.

"Can I help you?"

"We're here to see Detective Roberts," I bit out, doing my best to curb my temper.

"Do you have an appointment?"

I inhaled for control. "He's expecting us."

Glancing away, he picked up a phone and pressed a button. Several beats later he spoke into the receiver. "There're two FBI agents out here for Roberts." He hung up the phone without waiting for a response and gestured to some chairs against the wall behind us.

"Have a seat."

I turned around in disgust, muttering obscenities under my breath, and settled on one of the hard plastic chairs. Joseph dropped into the one next to me. "Let it go, Nat."

This was how it always went when we entered a local cop shop. Most thought we were stepping on their toes when it came to investigations and treated us with contempt. It shouldn't bother me after all these years, and most times it didn't. Today, though, it bugged the shit out of me. My fuse was ever shorter lately. Leave it to Joseph to know exactly how I was feeling.

We waited so long for someone to come that I was seconds away from storming back over to Officer Hopkins when a man in a suit rounded the corner and made a beeline for us.

With an outstretched hand, he greeted us. "Sorry for the wait, gentleman. I'm Detective Roberts."

Joseph shook his hand first. "No problem. I'm Agent Crocker. This is Agent Morgan."

I gripped his hand as he responded. "A pleasure. Now, if you'd like to come with me, I'll let you take a look at the letter Ms. Parrish received. Then, you can speak to her if you'd like."

The detective led us down the hall past several offices and an interrogation room before entering a conference room with a large, rectangular table in the center. At the near end of the table, in a clear plastic evidence bag was a sheet of plain white stationary with words printed across it. I reached it first, carefully picking it up off the table. My eyes scanned the contents of the letter, each word spreading dread through me. We'd need to take it to our lab to analyze, but from my personal knowledge of the case, and each and every prior letter found, this sounded exactly like one written by Casanova. *Fuck.*

"Now normally we handle this kind of thing on our own, but the Chief has been following this case since the beginning. He knew you Feds have been in charge of the investigation for the last couple years or so. Ever since it crossed state lines. He's the reason I called you all."

Casanova was the name we'd coined for the suspected serial killer. At last count, he was credited with the murder of five women between the ages of thirty-five and forty, all brunettes, with blue eyes and small-built body frames. Each one was a businesswoman with varying career choices including an administrative assistant, a paralegal, a lawyer, a CEO of a small business, and a doctor. None of them knew each other in either a professional or personal capacity.

The first death was reported three years ago. The second, six months later. Each death came almost exactly six months after the last one. Joseph and I had been pulled onto the case after victim number two, Leslie Peterson, who had been found in a wooded area along the Pocomoke River near the Eastern shore of Maryland with her heart cut out. All five women had reported receiving anonymous 'love letters' and all had been butchered with the same M.O.

I passed the letter over to Joseph to get another opinion. While he read the letter, I turned to the detective. "Tell me about the vic."

"Her name is Dr. Madeline Parrish. She's some head doctor who relocated here a couple weeks ago. She reports that she began receiving flirtatious 'love letters' about six months ago, but in the last month or so they've become a bit darker and ominous. Her words. The last letter she received, until yesterday, was three weeks ago. A week before she moved here."

With every word Detective Roberts spoke, my muscles tightened. I could also feel the tension radiating off Joseph. No fucking way?

"We'd like to speak with Dr. Parrish." Joseph stepped in when words clogged my throat.

"Sure thing. Follow me if you would."

With letter still in hand, the detective led us out of the conference room and back the way we came, stopping at the interrogation room we'd first passed. He opened the door and we followed him in. Joseph slammed into me when I drew up short, and I rocked forward on my toes before gaining my balance. *Son of a bitch.* I heard him mumble "shit" under his breath behind me, which jerked me back to attention, and I continued moving into the room to allow my partner entrance.

Madeline's expression of utter shock and mortification was obvious. Quickly though, she cleared all emotion from her face and sat perfectly poised in the rusted metal folding chair, her white-knuckled hands resting on the table the only sign of her agitation. Roberts closed the door behind us, and his gaze darted questioningly between us and the woman I hadn't been able to get out of my head. I ignored him.

Continuing as though my entire axis hadn't just shifted, and ignoring the speculative glare of the detective, I calmly nodded in greeting before introducing myself. "Dr. Parrish, I'm Federal Agent Nathaniel Morgan and this is my colleague, Agent Joseph Crocker. We'd like to ask you a few questions, if that's alright."

"Of"—she fisted her hand over her mouth and cleared the gravel from her throat—"of course."

While Roberts stood in the corner, we took a seat; me across from her and Joseph at the head of the table to her right facing the door. He laid the letter on the table and when her eyes dropped to it, all the color left her face, leaving her looking like she'd seen a ghost.

There were so many questions I wanted to ask. The least of which included the fucking letter that suddenly seemed to be burning my fingertips even though I no longer touched it — but the others would have to wait. The current situation was most important and needed to be dealt with first.

The Dom in me warred with the agent in me. For the past six years I'd been a no-nonsense, some might say callous, investigator. But, knowing this was Madeline, I wanted to both protect and spank the hell out of her for putting herself in possible danger by potentially ignoring these letters for so long. I needed to find a way to meld the two cohesively. Joseph was always the gentler one of us. The one who put everybody at ease. I didn't think I knew how. For Madeline, though, I needed to try.

"I understand from the detective that you recently moved to the D.C. area. Can you tell us what brought you here?"

She shifted slightly in her chair. Not like she was guilty of something, but like she was uncomfortable sharing her reasons. It made me want the answer all the more. Reining in my patience, I waited until she was ready to speak.

"My… boyfriend and I broke up a few months ago, and I was ready for a change of scenery. I was also fed up with these letters. I assumed once I was no longer around, they would stop. But this one is different than the rest. There's almost an angry tone to it. Like he's annoyed that he had to track me down."

I'd caught Madeline's earlier pause and wondered if she'd actually meant Dom. It was definitely a question I would be asking later. In private. And there *would be* a later.

Joseph jumped in with the next question. "You said *he*. Are you sure the author is a man?"

She nodded and straightened confidently. "I may not be a criminal profiler, but I *am* a clinical psychologist. I've been studying the human brain for over fifteen years. The way people think, feel, and act. There is a distinct difference in tone and specific word usage between a man and a woman. Yes, the prose seems flowery, but the words themselves are not. If you actually filter through the letters, they come from a more sexual than emotional place. They're definitely written by a man."

"When did you receive the first letter?"

She turned back in my direction. "The first letter I ever received was on March 3rd. I was working late that night and on my way out of the office. I spotted it on the floor in the waiting area of my practice. I don't know how long it had been lying there, and since my secretary hadn't brought it to me when she left, I assume whoever delivered it slid it under the door."

"Were all the letters delivered the same way? Anonymously to your office? You didn't install video cameras, considering how long you say you've been receiving them?"

"Nat," Joseph practically growled in warning next to me. I couldn't help the delivery of the last question, and everyone in the room, most notably Madeline, could hear the frustration, and terseness, in my tone.

"No, I never installed video cameras," she responded with slight sarcasm. "At least not on the floor where my office was. I was protecting the privacy of my patients. I believe the building itself has surveillance cameras, at least outside and most likely in the lobby. However, it's a large, heavily-trafficked office building with over twenty businesses housed inside. There was no way to pinpoint who was going where. But, to answer your question, yes, they were all delivered to my office."

She paused and all traces of sarcasm vanished. I could tell she was remembering something because her body began to tremble, and her voice shook slightly when she continued. "Until this one."

My hackles rose when I saw how visibly spooked she was now. "Where was this one delivered, Madeline?" I barely noticed my slip from professional to personal. I only knew my need to protect and keep my submissive safe from harm was flaring to life. Every protective instinct was firing at the moment. They erupted when she finally answered my question, her voice barely audible.

"It came to my home."

CHAPTER 8

adeline

When Nathaniel walked through the door of the interrogation room, my stomach dropped in shock. Joseph stepping in right behind him had it jumping back up into my throat and my heart almost beat out of my chest. Once both organs finally settled, my natural instinct was to rush into their arms for comfort. Which was crazy. Just because we'd played at Black Light didn't mean they were my Doms. I was blowing the connection I thought I'd felt way out of proportion. I was taking my feelings of loneliness and creating an irrational relationship that didn't truly exist. It couldn't. I mean, I didn't even know these men. People didn't fall that fast for each other. Not in real life at least.

"—eline."

I blinked back to attention when I realized I missed something. "I'm sorry, I didn't hear you."

Joseph spoke from my right. "I asked if you had noticed

anyone unusual hanging around your neighborhood? A parked car that didn't belong? Maybe a van with a logo of a company you didn't recognize?"

I searched my brain again, even though the detective had already asked me these exact questions. I told Joseph the same thing. "Not that I can recall. I haven't been in the city long enough to make friends with my neighbors, and I'd have no idea if a company was real or not. I'm sorry, but there's nothing more I can remember."

"Was the letter found outside the home or inside?" I turned back to face an intimidating looking Nathaniel in front of me. My hands shook as I recalled the feeling of terror at seeing the letter on my kitchen counter. I felt violated. This... person had invaded my personal space. My office had been bad enough, but to know that he'd been inside my home? It made my skin crawl. The clearing of a throat brought me out of my daze and I realized they were still waiting for an answer.

"Inside."

Nathaniel turned in his chair to speak to Detective Roberts. "I assume your officers have already been to the house and dusted for prints and checked the perimeter for any signs of recent activity."

The detective stepped forward from his position against the wall. "Yes. The house came back clean. No prints or sign of forced entry."

"What about outside? Near the windows or back door? Any signs of footprints or disturbed brush or broken limbs on bushes? Anything that might indicate point of entry?"

Roberts' face took on a pink hue. "I'm not sure."

I could see the tension in Nathaniel as he stood and stepped toe-to-toe with the officer. His voice was gravelly. "What do you mean you're not sure? You have a threatening letter, potentially from a serial killer, so you sure as hell better know whether you checked the property for evidence."

My brain grew fuzzy as it zoomed its focus in on those five syllables. A buzz sounded in my ears and my vision dimmed. I forced my breathing to slow and I blinked it all away. My voice cracked when I spoke barely above a whisper. "Serial killer?"

Still, Joseph heard me because his hand covered mine. My eyes darted up to meet his and there was so much reassurance in their ocean blue depths that I could feel myself breathe the tiniest bit easier.

"Everything will be okay, Madeline." He smiled convincingly at me.

I turned my hand up to clutch his. For some reason, my heart actually believed him. My brain wasn't too sure though. I glanced up at Nathaniel, who was looking down at me, and his face held the same expression Joseph's did. Like everything would be all right. That nothing, and no one, would harm me on their watch. Our connection was broken when he turned back to Detective Roberts.

"I'm going to make a call to my director. We'll be sending field agents to Dr. Parrish's house to examine the areas your team missed. While we appreciate the time and effort the Arlington P.D. have taken so far, your involvement in this case is finished. My colleague and I will be taking over this investigation. We'll call if we need anything."

Roberts bristled at the announcement, but gave a brief, curt nod. Nathaniel and Joseph rose together.

"We'll need to examine the crime scene as well. If you don't mind, Dr. Parrish, I think it would be best if we head there now while everything is still fresh." There was a hint of steel in Nathaniel's tone that made me realize he really wasn't making a request.

"Of course."

"We'll escort you to your vehicle and follow behind."

I gathered my purse and made my way to my car. I could feel the heated glances of the two men behind me. Neither of them spoke and I certainly wasn't going to start up a conversation. My gaze continuously darted up to the rearview mirror on the drive home, the reflection of the men following me making my stomach queasy the entire ride. I still couldn't get over the shock of seeing them walk into that room. My mind kept wondering what they were thinking. I hadn't been able to get a solid read on the entire situation during their questioning. Were they now regretting our time at Black Light? Did they still want more? Did *I* still want more? Was there really a serial killer out there sending me these letters? Each mile made me more nauseated.

I hated this uneasy feeling.

By the time I pulled into my driveway, my stomach was completely knotted up and I was a bundle of nervous energy. I didn't wait when I exited the car and walked to my front door. Unlocking it, I went inside, leaving it open for the men following behind me. I stepped into my living room just as I heard the door click shut. Inhaling for courage, I turned and faced the two imposing men taking up way too much room in my house.

Lord, just the sight of them had my body heating and my knees quivering. They were like night and day. Nathaniel was a force of nature, while Joseph was the calm that followed. Yet I responded to them equally. Hating the silence, I broke it. "Would you like something to drink?"

Joseph prowled forward, his thick, muscular body moving fluidly to shorten the distance between us. When we were toe-to-toe, I couldn't help but flinch when his hand came up. He merely palmed the back of my neck and pulled me to him, his free hand gripping my hip. Instinctively, my arms circled his waist, and I breathed in his comforting scent. I didn't realize how tense I was until I was in Joseph's embrace. Then, it was like he was absorbing all my tension, because every muscle relaxed and I melted into him.

"How are you feeling?" His voice rumbled through my chest.

I looked up at him and tried to pull back slightly, but he

refused to let me go so I stopped trying since I was where I wanted to be anyway. "Shook up. Violated. You name it, I probably feel it."

"I think it's best if you move to a safe house. At least until we figure out who this person is."

I vehemently shook my head. "No. I left North Carolina because of this guy. I refuse to run anymore. I'm not leaving my home."

"Mad—"

I pushed back harder, and this time Joseph let me go. With hands on hips, I stood firm in my response. "I said no. I'm staying here."

"Then you'll have a protective detail stationed out front and have some damn surveillance cameras installed this time." The directive came from Nathaniel, who'd moved farther into the room. He now stood beside Joseph, his eyebrows dark slashes accenting an expression that sent tingles through me. There was such a primal fierceness to him. I was also a little disappointed at the distance he maintained.

I acquiesced to his command. "Fine. But I'm not putting cameras in my office. I won't do that to my patients."

He accepted my compromise with a nod.

"The ERT should be here soon to comb the outside of the grounds in search of evidence."

"ERT?"

"Evidence Response Team."

I nodded. "Ah. Well, tell them to be careful of my babies, please."

They looked at me questioningly.

I flushed a little self-consciously. "I have a large flower garden out back that I adore and take care of. It's what I do to de-stress and the primary reason I bought this house. So, I would appreciate it very much if they didn't trample and destroy my hard work. Above all my lilies. I transplanted them from North

Carolina, so they're still fragile. And considering it's fall, they won't bloom much longer."

"I'll make a note of it."

"Thank you."

I hated how stilted our conversation was. There was so much awkwardness that hadn't been present when we'd been together at Black Light. It also made me question the protective display from Joseph moments ago. I shifted nervously.

"If there's nothing else then?" I attempted to side step around the men, leaving the question hanging. My anxiety was getting out of control and I needed to rein it back in. I didn't make it far before a strong hand lightly, but firmly, clasped my upper arm. I stared down at it for a moment before following the line of it up and colliding with a pair of smoldering, coffee-colored eyes. The heat from Nathaniel's touch spread down my arm before settling deep inside me where my core tingled and burned with fire.

"Do you really think you can dismiss us so easily, pet?" he growled low in his throat and his grip tightened just slightly. Not enough to cause me pain, but enough to get my full and complete attention. Not that he didn't already have it. I briefly stared into his mesmerizing eyes, but true to my submissive nature, a single raised brow had my gaze automatically lowering.

"I wasn't necessarily trying to dismiss you. I'm just feeling... unsettled."

Nathaniel's grip loosened and his thumb now stroked my skin, gently sending tiny sparks tingling through my arm.

"Unsettled about what?"

I hesitated too long for his liking, because the stroking stopped and he spoke with a warning tone. "Madeline."

I almost huffed out an annoyed breath, but caught it before it escaped. Something told me now wasn't the time to act like a petulant child. "Everything. The letter. You two. I certainly wasn't expecting to see you today. Especially in this capacity. It threw me for a loop. I just wish I'd been more prepared."

A touch to the small of my back startled me. I hadn't realized Joseph had moved closer. Now that I was paying attention, I realized I was fully surrounded by their heat. Nathaniel at my front, Joseph at my back. I should have felt overwhelmed by their presence, especially so far inside my personal space. Instead, I felt comforted and protected. It was a heady feeling. One I wanted to continue.

"If you were shocked, how do you think we felt walking in and seeing you? Knowing that the same submissive we'd played with, one we can't get out of our heads, may be receiving letters from a suspected serial killer?"

I shuddered again at those two words and the men stepped even closer, caging me inside their embrace. I couldn't keep the fear out of my voice. "Do you really think my letters are from your suspect?"

Joseph's hand shifted from the small of my back to cradle my hip, offering a comforting squeeze. "We won't know for sure until our forensics team analyzes the evidence, but based on what I saw, I have my suspicions it's from our serial killer."

"I don't get it. I mean, I've been getting these letters for six months. He's never attempted any more contact beyond that. If the person writing my letters and this Casanova person are one and the same, why hasn't he made a move yet? Not that I'm complaining. I just don't understand."

"Maybe he has."

I turned to stare at Joseph in fear. "What do you mean?"

I felt his hesitation, like he was now regretting speaking up. I wouldn't take silence for an answer. He must have sensed that, because he answered my question.

"Unlike the rest of the letters, you found this one *inside* your house. I think that's his first move."

I stepped away from him and wrapped my arms around myself. I knew I was being stubborn by staying here, but this was my new home. Even as a child I'd always been one to stand up to bullies. It wasn't in me to back down. I wasn't going to let this unknown person push me out of my own house. Still, a shiver raced across the back of my neck and the hairs on my arms stood up.

"He's coming for me, isn't he?"

CHAPTER 9

$\mathcal{N}$athaniel

IT TORE ME UP INSIDE SEEING MADELINE SCARED. I FELT POWERLESS and out of control especially knowing that fucking psychopath may have her in his sights. I cupped her face and stared down at her with an intensity I hoped seared itself on her soul. "We'll find him, Madeline. Trust us to protect you."

The timeline added up though. He hadn't been silent the past six months. He'd just relocated. And unless his M.O. changed suddenly, which was highly doubtful, our time was ticking. Each new victim had been killed around every six months like clock-work. If her letter writer was truly Casanova, then time was ticking, but there was no fucking way I was going to let anything happen to her. My Dom side wanted to take control. Now was not the right time though. Not with the field and tech teams on their way to her house. But soon. In the meantime, I needed to give her something to think about besides her fear. It was time for a reminder of what was to come.

I moved my hand from her cheek and threaded my fingers through her hair, tightening my grip until I was fisting the silky strands. I tugged her head to an angle and leaned down to bite the sensitive spot where her neck and shoulder met, her sharp inhale signaling arousal. An emotion so much better than her previous one as I rasped into her ear. "If our team wasn't currently en route, and it wasn't imperative that we ask you more questions, I'd bend you over this chair and spank your ass so hard you'd feel it for days. Maybe then you'd think twice about not taking more safety precautions."

Madeline's response was a fevered moan and she shivered under my touch. "I'm sorry, Sir."

I bit her harder and she whimpered at the same time her knees went weak, but Joseph and I caught her. "I thought I told you to call us Master."

"I'm sorry, Master."

A knock on the door interrupted us, and I growled in frustration before releasing Madeline's hair. It took her a second to recognize the sound, but when she did, she blushed furiously and stepped away from us, which I wasn't happy about. She attempted to straighten her finger-mussed tresses without doing a great job, but was still presentable enough that unless someone took a wild guess, they'd never know what we'd been doing. I gave her one more assessing look before stepping over to the door to let our team in. As I turned I saw Joseph speak lowly to her. Then, he moved to join me. Three field techs followed by two IT techs entered the house.

Joseph took the lead. "I'm going to assume that Reynolds filled you in already, but we're going to go over it again. Ms. Parrish has received a suspicious letter resembling one that we believe is from Casanova. Arlington P.D. has processed the inside of the house, but we're going to assume they've done a sloppy job. They also failed to process the outside properly. Most likely too much time has passed and any potential evidence has been contaminated, but we still need to be vigilant. The entire house, inside and out, needs to be processed as though it's a fresh crime scene."

I jumped in at this point, because I wanted the team to understand how serious I was. "Ms. Parrish has chosen to remain here instead of being moved to a safe house. Therefore, I need your best security cameras placed around the perimeter of the home as well as inside. Also, be careful of the flowers in the backyard garden, especially the lilies. Don't fuck them up."

One of the newer field techs looked at me in pure terror and Joseph coughed beside me. I didn't give a shit. Those flowers were important to Madeline, and I'll be damned if some careless idiot ruined them. Not if I could prevent it. It was my job as her current Dom to take care of her and the things she cared about most. When they all continued to stare at me, I barked out an order. "Get your asses moving!"

Like cockroaches scurrying in the light, everyone scattered, leaving the three of us alone again.

"Jesus, Nat." Joseph half-laughed, half-choked out.

I shrugged, unapologetic, because I knew what he was harassing me about. "They're not paid to like me. They're paid to do their job and do it well. Besides, this is for Madeline. Do you want anything done half-assed? I didn't think so."

When I turned on my heel to face her again, she'd covered her mouth with a hand and her eyes were shiny with unshed tears. "Thank you."

"You're welcome. Now, we need to ask you some more questions. See if we can come up with even one suspect. Are you up for it?"

"Okay."

"Let's have a seat." I gestured to the couch.

She toed off her shoes, settled into the corner of the sofa, and hugged her knees to her chest. Joseph took a seat on the wingback chair while I remained standing. I was too keyed up to sit.

"First off, have you kept the letters you've received?"

She shook her head. "None except the one I gave to the detective and the one I'd given the police back in Pinegrove months ago. I didn't think there was any reason to. I mean, they were harmless really. There weren't any threats. I just figured they were from some pervert getting his rocks off. Yes, they made me uncomfortable, but I didn't feel particularly threatened by them. In my line of work, I've gotten weird letters from both former and current clients before."

"Have you considered that one of your clients may be the culprit?" Joseph posed this question.

"Of course. But the tone of the letters doesn't match any of my clients. Current or former. I'm well versed in my client's mental health issues and not a single one of them presented with this kind of unhealthy infatuation. Nor with this level of psychosis. Most of my clients are dealing with PTSD or emotional recovery from an abusive relationship. I have a couple who demonstrate sociopathic tendencies, but not to this degree."

"That doesn't one-hundred percent rule out a patient."

Madeline sighed. "Nothing is a complete guarantee, but I feel pretty strongly about this."

"What about former Doms? Or perhaps someone you talked to at your local dungeon. Maybe you met him at a munch?" Joseph continued with his questions.

She shook her head. "No, none of those. The club was exclusive and every member was thoroughly screened. I didn't typically attend any munches and I've only had three long-term Dominants since I entered the lifestyle. I trust all of them with my life. Again, none of them presented with the psychotic tendencies displayed in these letters. I'm sorry."

Fuck. This was getting us nowhere. I wasn't pissed at Madeline, just the situation.

I crossed my arms and stared down at her. "We're still going to need the names of those Dominants. I understand that you trust them, but at this point we need to be investigating everyone. We may also need to speak with your former patients."

"I'm sorry, but I can't allow that." Her denial was vehement.

"Mad—"

"No," she declared firmly. "I spent years gaining my clients' trust. They've all made amazing progress towards their recovery goals. I'm not going to jeopardize my relationship with them or compromise their confidentiality. You'll just have to trust me."

My jaw ached from clenched teeth, so I forced myself to relax. I could understand where she was coming from, and I was actually impressed with her integrity and professionalism, but it still didn't make me happy. I couldn't force her to give us the information. Not without a court order anyway, and I knew that would be the end of any further exploration of our connection. Selfishly, I didn't want to risk it. So, for now, I was going to take her word for it. But if for one second something changed, I was willing to take the chance and piss her off by getting that subpoena. "Fine, but I can't promise I won't force the issue."

She opened her mouth to retort but was interrupted by someone clearing his throat. Robbed of her voice, her narrowed-eyed glare made her feelings perfectly known.

One of the ERT guys stood in the doorway.

"What?" I barked out.

The man stuttered, but quickly shut his mouth. He composed himself before beginning again. "We've almost completed processing the outside of the premises, sir, but it's taking some time. The team is being cautious of the flowers. Once it's finished, we'll get started on the interior."

"Well, do it then." Frustrated that we weren't going to have the much-needed talk with Madeline, I was harsher than I should have been. God, I really was an asshole.

She didn't say anything, but I saw a questioning frown on

Madeline's face and a twinge of guilt passed through me — but I ignored it.

"I hope I'm not going to be next on your shit list."

I turned and fiercely glared at a tech guy I only knew as Kurt. It was a fucking circus in here, and I was ready for everyone to get the hell out. Non-plussed, he merely returned my look with a bored one of his own. Interesting. Usually I terrified the IT geeks. "We installed a motion detection floodlight and the guys will place security cameras at the back of the house, both sides, as well as the front once the ERT finishes. We'll also be installing a doorbell cam."

"Thanks Kurt," Joseph replied.

He turned with a nod and disappeared out the front door. We shifted back to face Madeline now that we were alone again.

"Are you sure we can't convince you to go to a safe house? We want to protect you." Joseph attempted one last time to get her to change her mind.

She hesitated, but then shook her head. "I know you do, but I can't run away. I trust you will do everything you can to find this guy before anything happens."

He sighed in disappointment, although I knew what her answer was going to be.

"Okay then. We're going to let the teams finish their job. Here's our contact information. If you receive another letter or notice anything out of the ordinary, I want you to call us immediately. Are you okay with the guys continuing to do what they need to do?" Joseph rose and handed Madeline one of his business cards. She had our personal cell phone numbers already, but this was official law enforcement work. I took that as my cue that we were leaving.

"Yes, I'll be fine. Thank you for everything you're doing. I know I'm not being the easiest person to deal with."

A gentleness I didn't even know I possessed compelled me to

cup the back of Madeline's head and drop a chaste kiss on her forehead. "We're going to be here for you no matter what."

I turned without another word and headed to the car leaving Joseph to say his goodbyes, as well as remind her of our date tomorrow, and to leave instructions with everyone. I walked straight past an open-mouthed and speechless team of co-workers who had just happened to enter the room unnoticed.

CHAPTER 10

 oseph

UNLIKE THE REST OF THE TEAM, NATHANIEL'S RESPONSE TO Madeline when we'd left her house yesterday hadn't shocked me at all. Like me, he couldn't get her out of his mind. I knew he'd been thinking of her all week, and we were both looking forward to seeing her again tonight. Before I'd followed Nat out, I'd reminded her that nothing had changed between us, even given the current circumstances. In fact, knowing she was potentially in the sights of this fucked up serial killer had us feeling even more protective of her.

We were both extremely unhappy with the fact she wouldn't move to a safe house, but at this juncture there was nothing we could do to persuade her. Yes, we'd played at Black Light, but she wasn't our collared sub, which meant that, unless we dragged her kicking and screaming, there wasn't much more we could do beyond making our displeasure known. With time, maybe she'd see reason and the need to please us might change her mind. We could only hope. In the meantime, I contacted our boss and requested a security detail be placed on Madeline, since we were confident the letter had come from Casanova. There was no mention of a safe house. Yet. He reluctantly agreed.

Nathaniel's parting kiss also required me to speak with the team. Short of threatening them, although we didn't have an ounce of leverage to use, there wasn't much I could do should they decide to go to our superiors about what they'd witnessed. Especially knowing they weren't particularly fond of Nat. I was the one always smoothing stung egos.

Which was maybe why I found it incredibly surprising when Kurt shrugged off the discussion. "She's probably safer being with you two anyway. I know you guys will do whatever it takes to protect her." I was a little floored by his nonchalant acceptance and non-judgmental attitude of the three of us together if the truth be told. The other guys were harder to read. There was a mixture of skepticism and envy in their expressions. Only time would tell if there were any repercussions from Nat's actions today.

I'd called Madeline a few hours after we'd left yesterday to check in and get the names of her former Doms. Nat's and my time today had been spent interviewing them as well as consulting with a handwriting and forensic document analyst. She confirmed the letter Madeline had received was a 99.9% match to every other letter written by Casanova. Which meant that she was, in fact, his next potential target. So long as he didn't deviate from his prior M.O., which statistically wouldn't happen, we were already at six months, which meant we needed to find him fast.

A glance at the clock told me that it was time to get ready to pick up our sub.

"I'm heading to the locker room for a quick shower."

Nat nodded absently, his focus on the computer monitor in

front of him. "I'll be there in a bit. I want to finish this last bit of research I'm doing on a Vincenzo 'Vince' Russo. He was Madeline's last long-term Dom. According to him, they broke up about three months ago. He was cagey about the reasoning though."

I heard the suspicion and, perhaps, envy. From our interview with Madeline at the station, I'd gathered she was still recovering from the breakup, although it had happened months ago. She didn't explain why they broke up or who was responsible for it. My fists clenched with the need to punch this unknown Dom for hurting our woman, because she was obviously still hurting whether she admitted it or not. I wanted to soothe her hurts. Like Nat, I was also curious about the reason for their breakup. "I'm sure Madeline would have told us if there was something suspicious about him. You're looking for something that isn't there."

He glanced up at me briefly before his gaze returned to his screen. "I'm ruling out potential suspects."

I shook my head. "If you need to know that bad why they broke up, then ask Madeline."

"Oh, I plan on it. Have no doubt."

Knowing how stubborn Nat was, I knew she was in for a serious interrogation. He may not have realized it yet, but he was starting to fall for her. We both wanted to know everything about her, but more so Nat. He hated secrets. He also despised lies. Knowing his past, it was completely understandable. They were the two things he couldn't forgive.

Leaving him to his obsessive researching, I headed to the locker room, anxious to see our angel again.

AT PRECISELY FIVE MINUTES BEFORE SEVEN WE PULLED INTO Madeline's driveway. Nat's hair was still damp from the quick shower he'd taken. Like me, he was wearing a pair of leathers with matching black leather boots. The fall nights were quickly turning cooler so we both wore long-sleeved shirts, but I knew the minute we entered Black Light, they would be coming off. Especially since we'd be playing with Madeline. My cock twitched at the thought.

Nat and I had talked on the way about getting some answers from our sub. I paused for a moment and relished in how easily I'd started thinking of Madeline as ours. It might take Nat a little longer to get there. I knew my best friend though, probably better than he knew himself, and there was no doubt he was heading in that direction.

"You feel it, don't you?" He looked over at me just as I started opening my door.

I glanced over my shoulder, knowing exactly what he was referring to. "I do."

He only nodded, accepting my answer, before heading up the walk to Madeline's door and knocking.

My sharp inhalation matched his growl when the door swung open and the vision appeared in front of us. As though to defy the angelic image she'd presented last week, tonight she was wearing a black dress. But not just any black dress. One with a v-shaped, plunging neckline spread so far apart half of her breasts were exposed before it tapered to a point between her belly button and pubis. The hem didn't even reach mid-thigh. *Holy fuck.* I was torn. Part of me wanted to bend her over, slide that tiny piece of fabric she called a dress up, and fuck that tight pussy raw. The other part wanted to drag her inside and make her change into something else so no one could see her body but us.

Madeline threw us a look that said she knew exactly how affected we were at the sight. Oh, the little sub thought she could tease us. Obviously she'd enjoyed last week's punishment so much she was ready for another and I was more than happy to oblige.

"You're enjoying making us fucking hard as a rock, aren't you pet? That dress should be illegal."

She giggled and twirled in a circle giving us the full view. The back matched the front with the tapered vee stopping just above her ass crack, and the hem hugged the curve of her ass. It was going to be a pleasure stripping it off her body.

"Do you like it?" Her hands smoothed the fabric down her belly and hips. "I've never worn it before tonight so I wasn't sure how it would look."

Beside me Nat let out a sound of pleasure. "Pet, if I liked it any more you'd have to beat me off with a stick. You're absolutely stunning. You'll be the envy of every woman tonight, because they know there's no comparing to your beauty."

While I stared slack-jawed at the poetic compliment I'd never heard from him before, Madeline blushed prettily and stood on tiptoes to kiss him on the cheek.

"That's so sweet of you."

He stepped so close to her there was barely an inch separating them and leaned down, his lips brushing against her ear. "Pet, there's nothing sweet about me. My only thought right now is using one of my knives to cut this so-called dress off you and thrusting so far inside that pussy my come will still be dripping out of you days from now."

She whimpered at his words.

He moved away, his fists clenched like he was fighting the urge to reach out. "Now, let's get going before I forget all about this concert and your watchdog on the street and drag you upstairs to fuck you ten ways to Sunday."

"Ready?" I offered her my arm. Immediately, she slipped her hand through the crook of it and did the same with Nat when he offered her his as well.

"We'll continue this at Black Light," he promised.

CHAPTER 11

$\mathcal{M}$adeline

"THIS IS RUNWAY?"

Wide-eyed I stared at the three-story building on the corner. Unlike the last time, there was no side street and psychic shop. Men wearing suits, whose arms were decorated with young women wearing elegant dresses, graced the front of Runway. Flashes from cameras held by ambitious members of the paparazzi vying for the best picture of whatever celebrity was here lit up the evening sky. Some posed while others tried to avoid the cameras altogether. A line of people stretched along the sidewalk waiting for their turn to enter the exclusive club.

Joseph nodded. "Yep. You probably haven't heard of them since they're more local celebrities, but the club was opened by two former models, Jaxson Davidson and Chase Cartwright. They caused quite a ruckus in the political world a couple years ago when they came out as more than just business partners. Mostly because Jaxson's father is a senator. Shit really hit the fan when they fell in love with Emma Fischer and the three of them formed a triad."

"I think I remember you mentioning their names last week. Sounds like they caused quite a stir."

Nathaniel chuckled from the front seat. "Oh, you have no idea. Things have settled down a little now that they're married and living in California."

We circled the block before coming back around and pulling up to the valet. Nathaniel handed the attendant his keys and both men held out their arms for me. I slid my hands through and clasped their biceps while they escorted me to the entrance.

Joseph leaned down to speak softly in my ear. "Remember, Black Light is entirely separate from Runway. Most patrons have no idea what goes on beneath their feet, which means that once inside, we don't discuss the dungeon below."

I nodded my understanding and we weaved through the crowd loitering outside the building and headed to a cordoned off section labeled VIP.

Nathaniel reached into his back pocket and pulled out what looked like a postcard, handing it to the bouncer who scrutinized it thoroughly.

"I need to see your identification please."

Both men retrieved their wallets and handed their IDs to the large, ridiculously cut man. He looked up and down between the plastic cards in his hand and the men on either side of me. His eyes then landed on me and an approving glint twinkled in their depths as he scanned the length of my body pausing briefly at my chest. Two identical growls raced along my nerves before settling low in my belly. Joseph and Nathaniel placed a possessive hand on my hip and did their best to position themselves to cover me.

The security guard merely smirked, obviously enjoying raising their hackles. He flicked their IDs toward them and removed the satin covered rope from the metal stand and let us enter. I hid a smile when he winked at me as we passed him. No need to rile up my men even more, no matter how much I liked the fact they seemed jealous. They had nothing to worry about in that regard. Mild flirting aside, I had no interest in anyone but them.

I couldn't withhold my curiosity. "What was the card you handed him?"

Joseph released his hold on me to open the door for us and we stepped through, Nathaniel's hand burning hot on my lower back.

"We won a special VIP invitation to Runway from a charity auction a few months ago."

"I'm glad the money went to a good cause."

"It did. A young local girl needed money for cancer treatments. Emma, Jaxson and Chase's wife, saw a flyer somewhere and contacted her mother to make a few donations. They ended up raising a little over $500,000 if I remember correctly."

"Wow, that's incredible."

We passed through security and then I finally got a look inside Runway. Holy shit, I was speechless as my eyes shifted back and forth and up and down as they scanned the interior trying to take it all in. A huge dance floor, already crowded with people, opened up in front of us leading up to the stage. The neon lights of the bar to our left drew my attention in that direction. Everything was glitz and glam. The place was utterly breathtaking.

"Let's get a drink before the concert starts."

THE CROWD ROARED AS THE FINAL NOTES OF THE ENCORE FROM THE popular rock band, *Crushing Stones*, echoed through the room before dying out. During intermission, Nathaniel and Joseph had shared that Jonah 'Cash' Carter, the lead singer, also happened to be a member of Black Light. They didn't know him personally, but they had seen him and his wife playing downstairs multiple times. This was also a rare appearance for them since they were touring to sold out shows. They'd only agreed to this concert as favor to Emma and to raise money for the charity.

"Did you enjoy the show?" Joseph leaned over and spoke directly in my ear in order to be heard over the noise.

I squealed in excitement. This was one of the best dates ever. "It was wonderful! I love their music so much. Thank you for bringing me to the show."

"It was our pleasure."

"You know what else would give us pleasure?" Nathaniel piped up, a wicked and devious grin gracing his face.

It wasn't hard to figure out what he was referring to, so I held back my laughter while still trying to feign innocence. "Oh, and what would that be?"

He reached out for me and tugged me along behind him with Joseph following hot on our heels. The three of us weaved through the crowd and around tables to the right of the stage. It opened up to an empty area with a back door to our left. Near the door was a tightly pinned curtain against the perpendicular wall. When we stopped in front of it, I started to ask where we were going when Nat placed a finger over my lips to silence me. Joseph scanned the area and when he tossed out "all clear" over his shoulder we quickly dashed behind the curtain.

"Why are we in a janitor's closet?" I stage-whispered, my eyes scanning the small room we stood in.

Instead of answering, Nathaniel pulled the mop that stood propped against the wall. A locking mechanism clicked and a door opened.

I only shook my head in amusement. "Good grief. This cloak and dagger stuff is crazy."

We headed down the neon-lit stairs, the door closing and locking behind us. Once we hit the bottom landing, we entered through a familiar looking door.

There, Danny, if I remembered his name correctly, stood

guard. Once we showed our IDs, paid my guest entry fee again, and finished stashing all our things in a locker, we set out to enjoy what I knew was going to be an incredible night. One that would define my relationship with these two Doms.

CHAPTER 12

oseph

WHEN WE STEPPED OUT OF THE LOCKER ROOM, I THREADED MY
fingers through Madeline's free hand. I'd noticed Nat hadn't
released his hold on her since the second he touched her upstairs.
Connected as a trio, the first place we headed once inside Black
Light was to one of the semi-private alcoves off to the right side
of the dungeon floor. I could feel the excitement humming
through my veins and all around us. We were all anxious to play.
The curtain to the semi-private room remained open. Nat got off
on people watching him.

"Strip," Nat ordered when we'd barely entered the room. His
already dark countenance darkened even further. His flirtatious
comment upstairs had been pushed aside and his Dominant,
controlling side was fully at the forefront, his energy now entirely
focused on his submissive.

Slowly, Madeline peeled each side of her dress down over her shoulders then gave a light tug to detach it from her breasts. She giggled at our expressions when she pulled strips of something off them. "Double-sided dress tape," was her only explanation. The dress slid off her hips to puddle on the floor before she stepped out of it.

"Wait," Nathaniel stopped her when she moved to bend down and pick it up. She halted and he knelt at her feet, picking up the dress to hand to me, and then he slid his hands down her calf prompting her to raise her leg. She balanced herself with a hand on his shoulder while he removed one heel, then her other. He set them off to the side before returning his hands to her legs, gliding them up her calves and higher when he rose to his feet again. He continued his trek, fingers lightly tracing the pink marks left behind by the adhesive she'd recently removed.

"This looks painful," he murmured in regards to the outline left on each breast.

Madeline's hair fluttered around her face when she shook her head. "No, not—"

Her words ended on a gasp when Nat bent and soothed the mark with his tongue.

"—really," she finished.

"Oh, it definitely looks like it hurts. I think I need to soothe your ache." He continued giving each breast his attention with lips, tongue, and fingers as he gently plucked at each nipple before gently molding her flesh.

"Will you soothe all my aches?" Madeline breathed out, a flirty tone in her voice.

Nat pulled back to stare down at her and paused. Then, in all seriousness he replied. "Every last one of them, pet."

There was a brief moment of silence as she absorbed his words and realized what he meant. He cupped her cheek and slowly lowered his mouth to hers. The kiss was gentle to start, but passions rose and Nat deepened the connection, his tongue plundering her mouth, learning her taste. Madeline wrapped her arms around him, her fingernails leaving moon-shaped divots in his back as she clutched him tightly to her, like she was marking him. I loved watching them together. It appeased the voyeur in me. It satisfied me deep down to see the spark between them. I knew there would be times when we'd all three be together and when we'd have our own time with Madeline. Tonight was about the three of us, but in this moment, it needed to be about them. We had plenty of time to explore.

Nathaniel raised his head, both of them out of breath. Madeline's expression was one of dazed arousal. He directed her to the bed and when she was settled he began removing his clothes. He shot me a glance that I took as my cue it was time. My heart rate accelerated even faster. I was more than ready to join the party. We planned on taking her to the edge, catching her when she fell over the side, and letting her spread her wings and soar.

I looked over at Madeline where she'd raised herself up on elbows to watch us disrobe. Her legs were slightly parted, and her wetness glistened on her thighs and pussy. Once naked, we set our pants and shoes next to her clothes. It struck me for a moment seeing our clothing laying together like that. It was such an innocuous thing, but it felt right seeing them tangled up, like our bodies would be soon. When I turned back, Nat had already made himself comfortable next to our sub. Again, their tongues dueled and his hand squeezed and molded her breast.

My eyes drifted down to her center. I wanted to lap up her juices like a man starved. My cock lengthened at the thought of being inside her. Her mouth had been amazing, and I knew her pussy would fit like a glove, but what I wanted tonight was to slide deep inside that ass. I wanted to watch my length disappear in her hole, stretching it wide, before pulling almost out and then opening her up again. Not wanting to wait a second longer, I joined the party.

I climbed onto the bed, pushing Madeline's knees up toward

her chest. I settled back onto my heels at her feet. My hands gripped her ankle and gently tugged, coaxing her to open further. She moaned into Nat's mouth and followed my unspoken command. Her lower lips were plump, pink, and wet with her slick juice. The small nub at the top was swollen and peeking out between the folds just begging to be nibbled on. Her asshole was exposed and I fisted my cock, squeezing it hard to distract myself from the sight. Soon that little hole would be stretched wide. In the meantime, I wanted to feast.

Madeline moaned and arched into my mouth when I leaned down and ran my tongue from anus to clit, stopping to suck on it and give it more attention. I wanted her writhing with the need for release beneath us. I wanted her begging us to fill her cunt and ass at the same time. A groan rumbled in my chest at the thought of her strangling my cock.

"Tell us about Vince." Nat's command was firm and come out of nowhere. Well, not really. I knew he'd been stewing on it since before we'd left headquarters to pick Madeline up tonight.

I glanced up when it took her a moment to react to his question. Her expression shut down and she tried moving away from our touch. Neither of us were having it. My grip tightened on her hips holding her in place while Nat fisted her hair even while he continued his assault on her breasts.

"Why did you break up?" He bit her nipple firmly, but not enough to cause harm.

"Oh, God," she gasped.

"It's Master, actually." He could be relentless when it came to getting what he wanted. And tonight, he wanted answers. Which meant that we were going to keep her on the edge of an orgasm until she gave him what he asked for. Once she did, the pleasure would be worth it. Until then, she was going to have to beg for release. After she answered his questions of course.

Adding to the sensual torture, I flicked my tongue across her clit. She whimpered with need, her hips bucking to seek more

80

contact. I smacked her pussy lips and she cried out at the sensation.

"Answer Nat's question and we may let you come. Otherwise, we'll continue denying you the thing you want most."

Madeline's skin glistened with sweat, her gorgeous face flushed with exertion, and her eyes were glazed with arousal. She was the most beautiful woman I'd ever seen.

"He couldn't give me what I needed," she let out on a gasp of air.

We were partway to the truth. Now it was time to get it all. My mouth lowered and I lapped at her cunt, licking and sucking, drawing her engorged clit between my lips and pulling gently on it. I grazed it with my teeth, then soothed it with a swirl of my tongue. She thrust up into my mouth, chasing the orgasm she was yet again going to be denied. I pulled back and she cried out.

"What did you need, pet?" Nat's words were muffled against her neck, but I heard them nonetheless. He punctuated his question by nibbling on the sensitive area in the crease. She cocked her head to give him better access, but ignored his second question. He pulled away and stared down at her, his eyes glowing with displeasure. Her eyes opened and she stared up at him dazed.

"I think we need to come to an understanding here. Twice now you've ignored my questions and for the most part I've let you get away with it. That stops right now. When I ask you a question you either give me the answer or you respectfully tell me to mind my own fucking business. But this silent treatment isn't going to fly with us. Now, I'm going to ask you one more time. What did you need that he couldn't give you?"

Madeline lowered her gaze and inhaled then exhaled, letting it out ever so slowly, I was guessing to either buy time or for courage. When she spoke, she did so quietly, and I missed whatever it was she said. Nat, however, jerked. *Oh, shit.* Maybe she told him to fuck off. But then his body relaxed and he gave her a look I'd never seen on his face before. It was one of such tenderness. He brushed her hair back from her face and laid his forehead against hers while they breathed in each other's air. Happiness unlike any I'd ever felt before flowed through me. Nat had so much shit in his past, he deserved love. Maybe more than anyone I knew. He was hard to love though. Mostly because he kept so much of himself locked away. He did it to avoid being hurt. Some people didn't take the time to look past his hardness. So, for him to connect so quickly and easily with Madeline made me happier than ever for the man who was like a brother to me.

"Say it again, pet. Louder this time so Joseph can hear you." His voice held a husky quality, like he was holding back some emotion.

Her gaze moved slowly between the two of us before stopping to rest on me. "It's you. He couldn't give me what I needed, because *you're* what I've needed. The both of you."

CHAPTER 13

$\mathcal{M}$adeline

NOW THAT I'D SAID IT, I COULDN'T TAKE IT BACK. NOT THAT I wanted to, because every word I'd said was true. They *were* what I needed. *Who* I needed. Apparently my confession was all that was needed to spur them into action.

"You're what we need as well. It's time we showed you." With those words, Joseph returned his attention to my pussy. He began nibbling on my clit sucking it hard inside his mouth, swirling his tongue around it. My hips bucked and he placed his arm across my abdomen to hold me in place as he continued his assault. I mewled in frustration. I needed more. My prayers were answered when two thick fingers pushed inside me, sliding in easily considering how wet I was. I could feel my juices slide down my crack.

My senses were cast into overdrive when Nathaniel's hot mouth encased my breast, sucking my nipple hard, his tongue flicking the tip sending tremors through me. I threaded my fingers through their hair, clutching their heads to me, not wanting to break the connection between our bodies. There was nothing I could do but feel. They touched me everywhere. Nathaniel's attention was divided between my breasts while Joseph continued his sensual attack on my pussy, his fingers thrusting harder and deeper. When his thumb flicked across my clit, the tension that had been building rushed through my veins from out of nowhere and exploded in a maelstrom of colors and lights. I cried out as the orgasm crested over me, my back arching and my whole body spasming from the release.

While I laid there, splayed out, my body utterly relaxed, I heard the crinkle of a condom wrapper. The bed shifted and then I was being pulled. I rolled and found myself on top of Nathaniel with my legs spread over his pelvis. Before I could take my next breath, he lined his cock up with my pussy and thrust, seating himself deep inside me. I put my hands on his chest and pushed myself up. Our eyes met and he palmed both my cheeks, his thumbs brushing back and forth across them.

"You're breathtaking, pet. I could look at you forever."

His words turned me the fuck on and I moved, rubbing against him, trying to create enough friction on my clit to bring forth another orgasm.

"Ouch," I yelped, my hand reaching back to rub my suddenly stinging ass. I turned my head to pout at my other Master behind me.

"No more orgasms until I'm fucking that ass of yours."

"Please hurry," I pouted and Nathaniel chuckled beneath me, the vibration traveling from his cock through my pussy and sending tingles reverberating inside me.

His answer was to spank me again. "Patience, angel."

I writhed in ecstasy when Nathaniel pulled me down for a kiss effectively thrusting his cock further up inside me and pushing my ass further up in the air. I wiggled when Nathaniel's hands shifted down to my ass and spread my cheeks wide open.

I jerked and then my body softened when I felt Joseph's tongue dart out and flick against my hole before rimming it. Nathaniel's tongue in my mouth mimicked Joseph's action. The duel assault had the tension building even higher. I moaned low in my throat when he speared it deep inside me, but his tongue wasn't enough. I wanted his cock.

Reaching back, I fisted his hair. "I need you inside my ass now. Please, Master."

Joseph took pity on me, because there was the sound of a drawer opening and closing and then moments later a cold wetness touched my back passage. Using two fingers, he coated the outside of my asshole with lube before pressing two fingers deep inside, spreading the lube around. He scissored his fingers, opening me wider, and I groaned at the sensation, relaxing my muscles allowing him further entrance.

When he removed his fingers, I clenched my muscles, effectively tightening my pussy's vice-like grip on Nathaniel.

"God, she's squeezing my cock. Fuck, yes."

I did it again, wanting to make Nathaniel feel as good as he was making me. The action turned him into a primal beast. He gripped my hips hard in one hand and rammed his cock deep inside me at the same time he grabbed the back of my head and slammed his mouth against mine. His kiss was feral like him. My entire focus homed in on his cock and mouth. So much so that I almost missed the feel of Joseph's cock pressing against my anus.

"Breathe in and out, angel," he rasped low in my ear.

When I exhaled, he slammed his cock home and I screamed in pleasure. Finally, they were both inside me.

"Fuck," he exclaimed. "You're amazing."

"I feel so full."

Then he began to move. Back and forth until Nathaniel caught his rhythm. He pushed and pulled, their hips moving in alternating movements. When Joseph retreated, Nathaniel advanced. They continued this coordinated dance of in and out before the rhythm changed again and they began thrusting together, each of them filling my cunt and ass at the same time. The tension grew when I clenched down and the fullness expanded. When Nathaniel reached between our bodies and rubbed my clit, that was all it took to send me over the edge.

I screamed out their names as my orgasm exploded through me, followed closely by Joseph's. Nathaniel continued thrusting until he threw his head back with his orgasm. Joseph pulled out and I whimpered in disappointment. A random thought flashed inside my head that I wanted to feel his come dripping out of my ass and mingling with not only my own slick wetness, but Nathaniel's seed as well. Fuck the thought was hot and sent more micro spasms through me. My pussy clenched again on the man beneath me.

Completely exhausted, I collapsed onto Nathaniel's chest, unable to move an inch. The bed dipped next to us as Joseph laid on his side. Bonelessly, I rolled off Nathaniel and collapsed in a heap between their two bodies. It was my dark-haired beast that gently brushed the sweaty hair back off my face.

"How are you feeling, pet?"

I smiled drowsily. "Like I've been fucked good and hard, Master."

He threw his head back and laughed, looking more relaxed than I'd seen him and ten years younger. "Then we did our jobs right."

Joseph leaned over and dropped a kiss on my lips. "I'm going to wash up in the bathroom quick then grab you some water and chocolate. I'll be right back."

"Close your eyes and rest, pet. I'll wake you soon."

I nodded sleepily and snuggled closer to Nathaniel.

CHAPTER 14

$\mathcal{M}$adeline

I BRUSHED AWAY THE LAST REMNANTS OF SLEEP, AND WHEN I shifted a low groan grumbled from my chest at the whole body ache radiating through me. It wasn't necessarily an unpleasant sensation, but only because flashes of what caused the sweet pain burst inside my head. My pussy and ass were sore, but in that throbbing, tingling aftermath kind of way.

I'd hit subspace hard and deep last night. My euphoria encapsulated me inside a bubble where only the three of us, Nathaniel, Joseph, and I, existed. I was floating safely in their arms, content in the dizzying joy of my release. Inside our safe space, nothing and no one could harm me. I was protected in the cocoon their strength provided. When I finally came down, they were there to catch me. I nibbled on chocolate fed to me from Joseph's fingers while Nathaniel kept me hydrated. I was on the verge of tears at the sweetness of aftercare. I didn't remember even leaving Black Light. The last thing I remembered before falling into an exhausted slumber was Nathaniel tucking the comforter around my naked form keeping my body warm and cozy. Hazy memories tickled my brain to also include the feeling of two sets of lips dusting across my forehead and whispered words I was having difficulty recalling now in the light of day. For some reason, I was desperate to remember.

Not wanting to get out of bed was overruled by the need to not waste my day. The busier I was the faster the day would go and then I would be able to see my men again. My heartbeat quickened at the thought. *My men.* A sense of rightness rushed through me, but I tempered it. There was such a connection between the three of us, more than I'd ever felt with anyone else, and I knew I was keeping a part of myself back, but it was out of self-preservation. I didn't want to get too attached and have my world come tumbling down around me. My heart hurt thinking about it.

I needed to put a stop to the negative thoughts bearing down on me, so I forced my aching body out of bed. My lilies were waiting for me. I knew it sounded insane, but I truly believed that my flowers recognized my voice and the love I bestowed on them. They always seemed to perk up when I tended them. The petals opened just a little further and while some might say it was the wind, I always felt like they leaned the tiniest bit in my direction when I passed by. Foolish, I know, but they were descendants of my great-grandmother Parrish's lilies that I helped her water when I was a little girl. She died when I was five and these bulbs were all I had left to remember her by.

I pulled my hair up into a messy bun and quickly showered. Once I'd dried off, I tore through my closet looking for my old tattered jeans and raggedy long-sleeve shirt.

I caught sight of my reflection in the full-length mirror and paused. Was that really me? I couldn't remember the last time I had this glow about me. This look of complete and utter contentment. I was actually... happy. I recalled the fire in

Nathaniel's eyes last night. They'd glowed fiercely, and bored straight into my soul, taking my breath away. It was like he was laying claim to me. Owning me. Possessing me. It was the same look in Joseph's eyes. I planned on reveling in their possession for as long as it lasted.

Shaking off the thoughts, I hurriedly dressed and headed downstairs for a cup of coffee. To my surprise, a pot had already been brewed and from the looks of it, it was still, if not hot, then at least warm. I hesitated for a moment when I spotted the sheet of paper, but smiled when I picked it up to read.

Good morning, pet. I thought you should know your couch is surprisingly comfortable. Also, I hope the coffee isn't too cold, or too strong, when you wake up. I made it right before I left, thankfully avoiding an audience. See you soon.

- N

I grabbed a mug and poured myself a cup. While it heated in the microwave I grabbed the creamer from the fridge. Once the hot brew was the perfect cappuccino color, I sipped the hazelnut-flavored beverage and peered out my kitchen window to the bright green, perfectly manicured backyard. I admired the various flowering plants growing with their multitude of colors. All the pinks, reds, yellows, blues, purples, greens, and seemingly every other color of the rainbow made me so happy inside. Every time a new flower bloomed it reminded me of new beginnings and all the beauty and wonder in the world.

I rinsed out my now empty mug and set it in the dish drainer before heading to the mudroom. The dirt smell inside reminded me of my grandmother and our times in her garden. I slid into my soil-stained tennis shoes and snatched up my gardening basket from the bench. The basket housed my gloves and all my tools, including my spade, shears, and other items. My feet attempted to lead me to my lilies, but since I typically spent the most time with them, I always saved them until last. Instead, I headed to my other flower friends.

Once I'd pulled weeds, snipped off dying buds and twigs, and watered the flowers that needed it, I headed over to my beloved lilies. Right before I reached them, I stopped short. Something felt off. I twisted right and left, my eyes darting around my yard, searching for... anything. Oddly, the air stilled around me like it too was holding its breath, not wanting to disturb whatever was out there. There was a sinister darkness closing in on me and my limbs felt heavy with a sense of impending doom. However, nothing moved. No shadows shifted. But even the leaves seemed afraid to dance in the light breeze.

You're being ridiculous. I shook off the uneasiness and continued the last few steps it took to reach the lilies. I stepped up to my favorite bundle and my foot collided with something. I looked down, but didn't see anything through the greenery. I squatted and parted the stems and leaves searching for the hard object I'd hit. At first I didn't process what I was seeing. Like a bolt of lightening my brain caught up with my eyes and a scream erupted from the depths of my throat. I stumbled and fell on my ass, scrambling backward and away from the gruesome scene like I was escaping a predator bearing down on me. My chest hurt from gasping in air that just wasn't entering my lungs. Black spots dotted my vision, but I blinked them away.

Needing to escape, I picked myself up off the ground and raced inside. I snatched up my cell phone from where I'd left it on the kitchen table and with trembling fingers pressed a few buttons. Forcing myself to take slow, calming breaths I tapped my fingers in a frantic beat on the counter, my eyes darting back and forth across the backyard through the kitchen window.

"Well, hello, beautiful." The sound of Joseph's voice calmed me some, but I was still freaking out. I thought I'd gotten my breathing under control, but when he said my name, I heard myself.

I was beginning to hyperventilate.

"Madeline, angel, I need you to relax. We're on our way. Just breathe, pet. Slow and steady. Deep inhale in, slow exhale out."

I heard his words, but my body wasn't cooperating.

"Madeline." This time, Joseph's sharp command filtered through my panic. I'd expected that tone from Nathaniel, but not Joseph. The even-tempered, almost mild-mannered one. It startled me, but it also had me listening. Now that I was, I could hear Nathaniel cursing at traffic in the background.

"Good girl. Concentrate on my breathing and follow my instructions. Breathe deep in."

We inhaled together before he spoke again. "Slowly let it out."

In time, our lungs deflated as we both pushed the air out. Joseph and I repeated our dance until, with agonizing slowness, my racing heart tempered its beat and my breathing evened out and became normal again.

"Better?"

"Yes, Sir."

He didn't bother correcting me. I think he knew I was still walking a tightrope and anything could send me tumbling over the edge.

"Now, tell me what's going on. Keep breathing, Madeline."

I inhaled a shuddering breath before finding my voice. With a hushed whisper, I answered him. "There's a dead body in my backyard."

"Over the lilies there that wave, and weep above a nameless grave!"
-Edgar Allen Poe, The Valley of Unrest

My dearest Madeline,

Did you find the gift I left for you? I know how important your garden is to you and that lilies are your favorite flower, which is why I put it there. I needed to make sure you received it. As I lay on the cold ground next to your gift, fingers laced behind my head as I stared at the stars above, I thought of you, Madeline. Of your long, caramel brown hair as it cascaded down your back, short tendrils curling around your face. I thought of your violet eyes, unlike any shade I've ever seen before, hidden behind your too-big glasses. They mesmerized me.

I pictured us waltzing together as I held you a little closer than required. Your hands and arms clung to me as I whistled a melody that echoed through the quiet surrounding us. The scent of the perfume wafting off the Oriental Lilies that bloomed so magnificently under the moonlit sky teased my nostrils as we moved in time around our own private sanctuary. No one would bother us here. We would be invisible to the outside world. Just the two of us.

And just as I leaned in to brush your lips with mine, your gift chose that moment to stir, to remind me where I truly was. The scream that rent the air pierced through my daydream, ruining the magical moment between you and me. I had no choice but to silence it. I wrapped my hand around its throat, cutting off the noise with a choked gasp. Have no fear, my dearest Madeline, it didn't suffer long.

Once it was over, I drew out my knife. As the blade pierced its skin, I again thought of you. Of your generous heart. And oh, how I wished it were mine. Soon, though, Madeline. Soon, it will belong to me.

I'm counting the days.

CHAPTER 15

athaniel

SON OF A BITCH. THE HORN BLARED AT ANOTHER DAMN CAR IN MY way. I slammed on the brake to avoid their bumper before jerking the wheel to the left and quickly accelerating past them, while Joseph remained on the phone with Madeline. I'd only heard his side of the conversation, but I knew Madeline was in trouble. We'd shared a smile when her number came across his caller ID, but when he'd barked her name, I knew something terrible had happened. It was killing me not to know what was going on. I laid on the horn again and got flipped off for my trouble. Fucking D.C. traffic. We needed to get to our woman now.

I fished my phone out of my pocket and tossed it to him. "Call the guard stationed there and let them know what's going on."

"Where are you now, Madeline?" Joseph continued questioning her while he punched the keys on my phone. I did my best to weave in and out of the crawling traffic on the Francis Scott Key Bridge, honking at cars to get the fuck out of my way.

What I wouldn't give for some damn blinking lights and a siren. Thankfully, we'd been near Georgetown so we didn't have to navigate downtown.

"Stay with me, angel. I'm calling the detail outside your house."

When the guard answered, Joseph barked out orders for him to go inside and wait for them to arrive.

He switched the conversation back to our woman. "Madeline, I need you to let the officer in. He's going to stay with you until we get there. We're close, I promise."

Finally, I hit Lee Highway and gunned it. In record time, I skidded to a halt in Madeline's driveway. Based on Joseph's tone, she'd calmed and didn't seem to be in any immediate danger, which made me feel only slightly better. I still wanted to murder someone.

Almost as a single unit, we dove out of the car and raced toward the door. Our feet pounded against the pavement and our heavy breathing echoed in the air. We practically flew up the three steps and landed on the front stoop just as the door opened. The moment Madeline laid eyes on us, she burst into tears and began to collapse. I scooped her up and with an arm behind her back and one behind her knees, I lifted her against my chest and carried her inside, leaving Joseph to follow and close the door behind us. My rage still burned brightly, but now that she was under my protection I was able to control it better. I whispered reassurances against her hair while I exchanged a glance and nod with Joseph.

While I settled a still-crying Madeline and myself on the couch, he escorted the guard outside to speak to him. I knew I needed to call our own forensics team in, but for a brief time, I needed to hold our woman. To know that she was safe. Her sobs slowed until she took in one last shuddering breath before raising her head to look up at me. She shifted as though to move off my lap, but I held tight, refusing to give up my hold. When she realized I had no intention of letting her go, she settled back into my arms.

She jumped and tensed when the front door clicked open, but relaxed when she spotted Joseph entering. His expression was one I didn't have difficulty reading, not after all these years working together. Anger, fear, and determination all radiated off him as he sat in the chair opposite Madeline and me. He leaned forward and rested his forearms on spread knees while he worried the fingers of one hand.

He heaved a heavy sigh as though not sure where to begin. "I questioned the officer. He says he didn't see or hear anything. I also contacted the ERT, who are on their way. I went out back, but didn't get too close to the"—his gaze darted up to briefly glance at Madeline before shifting his vision to me— "body, but from what I could tell, it appears to be a woman. I couldn't see much beyond her feet, and I didn't want to contaminate the scene."

"Fuck," I cursed, tightening my hold on the woman in my lap when I felt her shudder. "He's changed his M.O."

"Wha...what does that mean?" Madeline stuttered, her voice shaky.

Joseph and I looked at each other before he answered her question. "Honestly, I don't know. He's never deviated from who we assume is his intended victim. At least to our knowledge. Each woman who's been killed had been the recipient of love letters. No one else, besides you, has reported receiving these anonymous letters recently."

"That you know of anyway."

I looked down at her. The look of terror was back on her face, and it pissed me off. I was ready to kill for this woman. To make this all disappear. "Listen and listen well, pet. We're going to catch this piece of shit if it's the last thing we do."

Madeline's hand came up to cup my smooth jawline. Her violet eyes studied my face like she was memorizing every aspect of it. "That's what I'm afraid of. What if it *is* the last thing you do? You just said he's changed his M.O. What if he changes it again and goes after you two? No one would expect it or see it coming. If that woman out there is any indication, this bastard isn't playing by anyone's rules but his own."

While I was happy to see the fear leave her eyes and the steel enter her tone, she needed to remember who was in charge here. "Don't worry about what he may or may not do. This is what we're trained for. We *will* catch him. In the meantime, you're going to a safe house."

Tendrils of hair fluttered when Madeline shook her head in denial. "I told you I wasn't going to be run off by this asshole."

In a flash, I flipped her over so she now lay on her stomach over my lap, my right arm splayed over her shoulder blades and upper back. My left hand came down hard on her ass, eliciting a screech from her. She kicked and struggled to rise when I began to rain slaps down, alternating cheeks so she felt the sting and burn over her entire ass. Soon, she was sobbing, but still squirmed trying to evade the blows.

"Stop struggling and take your punishment like a good submissive or I'm going to add more infractions to the list. You won't enjoy what comes next."

"I'm not enjoying this," she spat out, but settled down.

"That's why it's called a punishment, pet." This came from the previously silent man across from us.

"Joseph," she begged, her eyes searching him out.

He merely shook his head. I knew he'd agree with me. "There are surveillance cameras surrounding your entire house and yet he still got this close to you and we never saw a fucking thing. It's no longer safe for you here and you need to recognize that fact. I understand you don't want to go to a safe house, which is why you're coming home with us instead."

Both Madeline and I froze, my hand suspended in mid-air. I certainly hadn't expected that, but it made sense. We were the best ones to protect her. It also gave us a chance to see if this... thing between the three of us was something we wanted to explore further. Maybe even take things to the next level. Joseph had said from the beginning that Madeline was 'the one' and I was almost starting to believe him. She was perfect for us in every way. But first, we needed to find and destroy Casanova. We had too much to lose now.

I loosened my hold on her now that her punishment was over and she'd calmed down. With tear tracks still staining her face, she gingerly sat on the couch next to me, wringing hands in her lap. I'd never seen her this unsure before.

"I'm scared." Her words were barely above a whisper and I had to strain to hear them. Joseph heard them loud and clear though, because suddenly he was kneeling in front of her, his large hands swallowing hers as he clasped them tightly. I let him comfort her, because he was so much better at the gentler stuff than I was.

"Oh angel, I know you are. We are too. Which is why you need to be where we can protect you."

"Nathaniel?" Madeline's eyes met mine. I wasn't sure what her question was. Did she think I didn't want her in our home? Or was there something else?

I shifted so my thigh made contact with hers, and I brushed my thumb under her eye catching a small amount of wetness left behind and wiping it away. "You know Joseph is right, pet. It's our job as your Doms to take care of you and make sure you're safe."

She nodded and opened her mouth, but her response was interrupted by the doorbell. Joseph released her hands and we both rose from our positions to let the team in.

THREE HOURS AND TWO POTS OF COFFEE LATER, THE FIELD TEAM had collected their evidence and our tech team ran a thorough scan to determine how Casanova had gotten past their security measures. That was something that was going into our report. If this fucker had the skills to bypass our cameras, then his hacker skills were top notch. Hackers of that magnitude left a footprint. They wanted the Feds to know they'd been bested. We may not know the identity behind their screen name, but they had a reputation in the hacker community. Hopefully that would help us find a single thread to trace and learn his identity.

The local medical examiner had also come and gone. The woman's body was transported to the county M.E.'s office where an autopsy would be performed to determine cause of death. Although, the fact that her heart was missing was a good indicator of what had killed her. Then again, there were indications of possible strangulation. Whether it happened peri- or post-mortem was still to be determined.

Throughout the evidence gathering, Madeline had merely alternated between pacing and fidgeting on her couch. She never sat still. Finally, everyone vacated the premises and the three of us were left alone again. Joseph and I took our respective positions on the chair and couch and waited patiently while Madeline continued pacing and worrying her lips. Patience had never been one of my virtues, and I'd almost reached my limit when she finally stopped moving and turned to stare each of us down, hands wrapped around her waist.

"You win."

I gave a mental fist pump, but I hated her wording. Like us 'winning' meant her 'losing.' The only thing she might lose was her life. Madeline needed to be reminded of that. Smoothly, I rose from my place and stalked toward her. She tried maintaining eye contact, but her innate submissive side had her eyes automatically lowering to meet the floor. I fisted her hair and firmly pulled her head back until she met my gaze. "This isn't a game, pet. There is no winning for any of us. Not until we catch this bastard. Even then, those women he killed... none of them won. So stop being stubborn and instead realize that this is the best option at the moment."

She blinked and her expression shifted until she looked sufficiently humbled. "You're right, I'm sorry. I've been incredibly selfish. Those poor women are dead and here I am worried about leaving my home and not letting this psychopath win. Please forgive me."

"There's nothing to forgive. You're a strong, independent woman, I get it. We're not trying to change that, but we"—I gestured between Joseph and me—"*need* this Madeline. We feel helpless knowing Casanova is out there, somewhere, mocking us. We need to feel in control. Having you near us is one way for us to accomplish that. So, let us."

"Yes, Master."

CHAPTER 16

oseph

"Pack whatever you think you're going to need for two weeks. We can come back later for anything you might have missed," Nat told her from his perch against the doorframe of her bedroom.

My eyes scanned her bedroom, trying to learn a little more about this woman who utterly fascinated us. A queen-size bed with a giant etched headboard graced one wall. There was a group photo of her and several other men and women on her dresser. All the furniture matched. It wasn't a hodgepodge of mixed pieces. Several books graced her nightstand, all of them looking like nonfiction research books, although she did have a collection of paperbacks in the bookshelf against the opposing wall. Everything was neat and orderly, with no stray clothes strewn about. Dirty clothes were in the hamper. Surfaces were dusted and polished. Between her job and home, Madeline was in complete control, which is why her surrendering to us was that much more intense. She got rid of everything and put it in our hands.

"I just need to grab my toiletries and then I guess I'm ready." She placed a large rolling suitcase a few paces from where Nat stood, then headed into the bathroom. He and I exchanged a glance. We both knew she didn't really want to leave, even if it was in her best interest. I considered telling her we'd stay here, but I wanted her away from this place. The chances of Casanova finding her with us were slim, and her safety was our main priority right now. Nat straightened up and I turned my head to see Madeline exit the bathroom, another small bag in hand. I shouldn't have been surprised by the size of it. She had this natural beauty that didn't need a lot of makeup or products to enhance it. He picked up the suitcase near him and left without a word. A flash of hurt crossed her face, but she quickly cleared it.

I moved next to her and held her free hand, my thumb rubbing along the length of hers. "He's worried and doesn't really know how to handle it."

She glanced up at me. "I'm not so sure about that. I got the impression he isn't too happy with me right now. Maybe staying with you isn't the best idea."

I tried not to let my personal opinion overrule my professional one, even if it was difficult. "Madeline, I know this is hard, leaving your home. I get it, really. Nathaniel and I just want you safe, and for the moment getting you out of this house is imperative. If you don't feel comfortable coming with us, no matter how much better we would *both* feel, then at least let us take you to an actual safe house. Someplace where Casanova can't reach you. I swear though, Nat is not angry with you."

She seemed to relax at my words, and I held my breath while I waited for the final decision from her. It would be a struggle, but we'd accept whatever decision she made, regardless. I'd make sure of it.

"I'll come with you." Her voice was firm and without hesitation.

"Smart choice, pet."

Madeline jerked and spun to stare at Nat who had approached without either of us noticing. I glared at him, but he didn't bother to glance my way.

"I'm not good with 'gentle' or 'soft.' Doubt I ever will be. But I'm pretty sure I've made it clear that right now your place is with us. That it's our right, our need, as your Doms to protect you. To provide for you. And you're going to be a good little sub and let us. Am I clear?"

She straightened her shoulders with confidence. "Yes, Master. Perfectly."

He nodded. "Good, now let me carry that bag."

Madeline handed it to him and, just like moments ago, he took it from her and disappeared without another word.

I threaded my fingers through hers and led her away from the bedroom. "C'mon, let's get you settled into your new place."

WHILE MADELINE PUT HER THINGS AWAY IN THE SPARE ROOM I'D shown her, I headed to the kitchen where Nat was pacing. I knew this without having to see it, because it's what he did when he was nervous. He paced. He always ribbed me about my purported belief in love at first sight. I didn't necessarily call it love. Just an intense feeling that there was this potential for "more".

When I'd first spotted her, my heart skipped a beat. For all I knew, she could have been collared. Or married. And that would have been the end of it. I would have been disappointed, but I would have accepted it. I knew Nat as well as I knew myself. Having Madeline in our house was more than nerve-wracking for him. I knew he was thinking about Elizabeth and the last time a sub lived with us. It had ended badly. That failure was a reminder to him, because this time, he was desperate for things to work out. No matter how jaded he acted, he also wanted that "more."

You didn't become someone's best friend without learning how he ticked. Nat had trust issues. Hell, knowing what I did about his past, who could blame him? He wanted to believe though. To go on blind faith that what he was feeling for Madeline was long-lasting. I still felt the burn of Elizabeth's betrayal, but I also still believed in fate. It was just going to take Nat longer to get there than me.

"It guts me that she really thought I didn't want her here. That I was angry with her," he said the minute I entered the room.

I grabbed a bottle of water out of the fridge and unscrewed the top. "She'll get to know the real you soon. Just give it time. You're rough around the edges, but I know how deeply you feel. You're my best friend. My brother. I get you. She will too."

He made a frustrated sound low in his throat. "I hope you're right, because I have no doubt I would fuck things up if you didn't have my back."

I couldn't help but laugh, because as much as I loved the guy, he was right. He probably would fuck it up. A low noise caught our attention. Madeline stood in the doorway wringing her hands and biting her lip like she wasn't sure she should interrupt.

"Come on in. You want some water? Something to eat? You're probably starving." I went over and slid my hand in hers offering her some reassurance.

"No, thank you. I don't think I could eat if I tried. Honestly, I just want to go to bed and forget this whole day ever happened." She shuddered and tears formed before she blinked them back. I had no doubt it was a trying day for her. It would be for anyone. Between the dead body and another note I'm sure Madeline was close to a breaking point. She was a strong woman, but knowing there was a serial killer out there targeting you would almost annihilate anyone.

"Why don't I run you a hot bath? Try to relax and then go to bed. Things will look better in the morning."

She nearly melted at my words. "Oh God, a hot bath actually does sound pretty amazing right now. Thank you, Joseph."

"My pleasure, angel. Come on."

CHAPTER 17

$\mathcal{M}$adeline

AFTER MY HOT BATH, WHICH HAD ACTUALLY HELPED RELAX ME, I'D gone to bed early hoping that it would help me sleep. Instead, I laid there for hours, unable to sleep. I couldn't shut my brain off. Instead, flashes of that poor dead woman's body kept me awake. Every time I closed my eyes all I could see was blood. I'd see her body and then suddenly it would morph into mine. I shuddered. There was no way I was going to sleep. Not like this.

I needed my men. Crawling out of bed, I grabbed my robe and slipped it on over my sleep tank and boy shorts. Opening my door, my feet instinctively took me to Nathaniel's room. Hesitantly, I knocked, and waited. Silence. I knocked again, this time a little louder. Nothing. I sagged in disappointment and turned to head to Joseph's room.

"Can I help you, pet?"

I yelped and spun around, colliding with the wall, hand on my chest trying to calm my racing heart at the disembodied voice. A shadow moved and Nathaniel stepped into the moonlight shining through the bathroom window. My exhausted body and mind chose that moment to expel all the shit I'd gone through over the last few months, and without warning I burst into tears.

"Fuck, Madeline, I'm sorry."

I barely heard Nathaniel's words over my sobs. Warm arms encircled me, pulling me close against his chest. I clutched his shirt like a lifeline, needing something to hold on to. I felt like I was drowning. Nathaniel shifted and his arms went beneath my thighs and then I was cradled against his chest, my arms wrapping around his neck while I bawled. There was a loud bang, like he'd kicked something. Then hinges creaked.

"Jesus, Nat, what did you do to her?"

"She was wandering the hall and I accidentally scared her when I was coming back from the kitchen. I didn't mean to." He sounded horrified.

"Come on, bring her in here."

Nat carried me further into Joseph's room and suddenly a light was turned on. Thankfully, my crying was easing off. I felt like an idiot. Even still I didn't move away. I felt safe in the strong arms that continued holding me tight. Bed springs squeaked when Nat sat down on the mattress with me on his lap. I felt another set of hands petting my head and I knew it was Joseph. Their calming touch was soothing me like nothing else. I hiccuped one final half-sob and then took in a shuddering breath. I lifted my face from Nat's neck and turned my head, resting it on his shoulder. My teary eyes met Joseph's worried ones and I sent him a watery smile.

"I'm sorry I overreacted. I'm so stupid."

"Don't you dare talk to yourself that way," Nathaniel's command boomed through my chest. "This was my fault. I should have known better than to startle you like that, however unintentionally. I apologize."

I merely nodded and scooted a little closer even though I was already practically plastered against him. He was just so warm. I didn't want to leave his embrace. "I know this may sound silly, but can I sleep in here tonight? I don't want to be alone."

Joseph's response was immediate. "Of course."

Nathaniel stiffened slightly underneath me before standing up and laying me on top of the covers. "Here, I'll get you all tucked in and I'll see you two in the morning."

I grabbed his hand, begging. "No. I need you too. Please don't leave me."

His expression softened and he palmed the back of my head, pressing his forehead to mine. "Don't worry, pet. I'm here."

I let out a relieved sigh.

"Come on, let's get you settled." This came from Joseph.

I shrugged out of my robe and handed it to Nathaniel. He carefully placed it on the chair and both men climbed into the bed, Joseph on my left and Nathaniel on my right. The light was turned off and the barest hint of moonlight filtered into the room. I rolled onto my side and curled up against Nathaniel who wrapped an arm around me. I reached back and found Joseph's hand. I gave a sharp tug and felt him roll. His warmth was nestled against my back, and I was sandwiched between them. Everything was going to be all right now. I closed my eyes and slowly drifted off to sleep.

"Good morning." I smiled sleepily at the man holding me tightly against him. I turned my head searching for his dark counterpart, but Nathaniel no longer occupied the bed. I pushed back the hurt and disappointment at his absence.

"Hello yourself, beautiful. How are you feeling this morning?"

I shifted. "Better than last night. I felt safe with you and Nathaniel."

Joseph kissed my forehead. "I'm glad."

I laid there quietly basking in this feeling of complete and utter awe that I was here, in this house, with these two men. I refused to acknowledge the circumstances, which brought me here. Instead, I was going to focus on the here and now. On my Dominants and how I planned on being the submissive they needed and wanted. Each day I was coming to realize more and more that maybe this wasn't a dream or make-believe. That maybe this was something special. Something strong that would last longer than a brief moment in time.

"Can I ask you a question?"

Joseph glanced down sensing the hesitance with which I asked. "Of course. You can ask either of us anything you want."

"When did you and Nathaniel start sharing women?" I snuggled closer to him avoiding eye contact, sighing a little when he brushed the hair off my forehead and stroked my face. My question didn't come from a place of jealousy. I was genuinely curious about their dynamic.

"I think it was about three years ago. We tried dating women individually, but it always felt like something was missing from the relationship. Nat said the same thing. Like the ebb without the flow. Which, I know, sounds weird"—he gave a short, unabashed shrug—"but there's a connection he and I have with a sub. It's not sexual between the two of us. It's just that a relationship doesn't feel like it's whole unless we're both involved in it. Once we realized that, we stopped trying to find a woman for each of us and instead, concentrated our focus on finding the right woman for both of us."

"I understand. Can I ask another question I've been a little curious about?"

Joseph tweaked my nose and smiled. "I already told you yes. There's nothing we won't tell you."

I studied his expression. He was so earnest, so I forged ahead. "Why do you and Nathaniel live together? I mean, I know you're best friends, but I would think you'd each have your own place."

He nodded as if understanding my curiosity. "We used to live separately, but once we knew that only a ménage relationship would fulfill our wants and needs, it made sense to start making a home for when we found our partner. It works for us."

The scent of coffee being brewed and bacon suddenly hit my nose and my stomach rumbled causing Joseph to laugh.

"Why don't you head downstairs for some breakfast. I have a couple calls to make."

He kissed me before I crawled out of the bed. I grabbed my robe off the chair and shrugged into it, belting it at the waist. Then I headed downstairs suddenly anxious to see Nathaniel.

CHAPTER 18

*N*athaniel

I KNEW THE SECOND MADELINE ENTERED THE KITCHEN. MY BODY buzzed with her presence. I cast a glance over my shoulder. Fuck, she was beautiful.

She paused a second when she caught my eye. "Can I help you with anything?"

I waved her off and gestured for her to sit down at the table. "Thanks, but everything is ready. Have a seat."

I plated the hot breakfast I'd made and walked over to where she sat sipping from one of the glasses of orange juice I'd already set out. I laid the plate down in front of her and smiled when she glanced up at me.

"Scrambled eggs and bacon are about the only things I know how to make that won't kill you." When I made to turn back to make my own plate, she laid her hand on my arm.

"I missed waking up to you this morning."

I caught the hurt in her words. "I'm sorry. I had some work to take care of and I didn't want to disturb your sleep. You looked so peaceful lying in bed."

"Thank you for taking such good care of me." The look in her eyes seemed to say that it had been a long time since someone had really taken care of her. It made me curious about the last Dom she'd been with. Even though she hadn't confirmed he was one of the reasons she'd moved here, I knew it was true given the information she'd provided us at the beginning of this case.

I threaded my fingers through her hair and palmed the back of her head before pressing a kiss to her forehead. "You're an easy woman to take care of."

Once my plate was full I returned to sit next to her. She took a few bites, but then pushed her food around on her plate.

"Food not to your liking?"

She jerked her head up and her eyes widened. "Oh no, I'm sorry. It's delicious. I was just thinking."

"Want to talk about it?" I set my fork down and looked at her with an expression I hope conveyed my genuine interest, because I really did want to know what was going on inside her head. Joseph was the patient and gentler one. Not that he was soft by any means, but he was better equipped to deal with... emotions. Emotions usually made me twitchy. But with Madeline, I was different. Or at least I wanted to be. I wanted to be the one she opened up to. To share her thoughts with. Her heart with.

When she hesitated, a single word spilled from my lips. A word I couldn't remember the last time I spoke. "Please."

"I was thinking about Vince actually."

Ouch. I guess I should be careful what I ask for.

She must have sensed my hurt, because she rushed on. "Not like that. It's just that when you said I was easy to take care of, it just reminded me of how hard Vince worked to take care of me and it always seemed like I was never satisfied, which makes me sound like such a selfish person. He did everything for me, was the perfect Dom, but it didn't seem to ever be enough."

"I don't think you sound selfish. I think you tried everything to make your relationship with him work. Sometimes, though, no matter how hard you care or how hard you try, it just isn't meant to happen. Some people are circles and some people are squares and no matter how hard you work to fit them together, it doesn't match up. Circles have to find other circles and squares other squares."

Madeline blinked and her tinkling laughter flitted through the room sounding like the sweetest song to my ears. "Really? That's your analogy of why my relationship didn't work with Vince? Because he's a circle and I'm a square?"

"Actually, you're not a square."

"So I'm a circle."

I reached for her hand and brought it up to my cheek. I turned my head and dropped a kiss into her palm. "You're not a circle either."

She swallowed and her voice was soft and questioning. "What am I then?"

"You're a diamond. Flawless and perfect. Strong. Crafted and molded specifically for Joseph and me. Besides, you said it yourself. He couldn't give you what you needed because he wasn't us."

Her eyes grew misty. Romance didn't come easy for me and normally I'd feel awkward and insincere spouting crap like that, but in this case I meant every word. Joseph was right, Madeline was meant to be ours from the moment we saw her. It didn't matter that we hadn't known her. She possessed an inner spark that ignited every fuse inside us.

"Can I ask you a personal question?"

I nodded. "Sure."

"I've seen you in work mode. You're... intense. Brusque. Terrifying at times. You give off this 'I hate the world' vibe. The only person who doesn't walk on eggshells around you is Joseph. That first night at Black Light I saw the darkness inside you, and I just wondered what makes you so angry all the time."

I was impressed by her insight. There *was* a darkness inside me, constantly trying to claw its way out. Joseph was closer to me than anyone. He was my brother. My family. The only one who could keep the monster on its leash. Until Madeline. She soothed the beast inside me. I knew my other colleagues thought I was an asshole, which was fine with me. I mean, I *was* an asshole, there was no denying it. The crazy thing was, no one had ever bothered to ask why. Except her and Joseph.

"Come with me." I gently pulled her from her chair and led her into the living room. Once seated, I settled her onto my lap. She laid her head on my shoulder and rested her hand on my chest, right over my heart. I soaked in the comforting gesture. It wasn't often I allowed anyone this close to me. Sex didn't count. That was most often about fulfilling a physical need. This right here, this embrace, was about intimacy, and that superseded bodies coming together for pleasure by far. This was about connecting emotionally and mentally with our submissive. Our woman.

"My parents divorced when I was ten. Two years later my father remarried. For the first year of their marriage, everything was fine. Denise mostly ignored me and my dad let her. He half-heartedly tried to encourage her interest in getting to know me, but he mostly gave up when she didn't put forth any effort. She wasn't cruel, but she didn't try hard to be nice. That was until my dad started traveling more often for work. Once a month he'd have to stay overnight in New York. Suddenly, she was making my favorite meals on the nights he was gone, letting me stay up past my bedtime, and asking me about my day. What we were studying in school. How I was doing in football practice. Then she started asking me if there was any girl I liked and if I had a girlfriend."

I sensed a shift in Madeline's posture and a change in her breathing. There was a new tension to her. I ignored it and continued speaking, my eyes unfocused on anything in front of me.

"My mom wasn't really in the picture so I soaked up the attention Denise was finally starting to show me. It was three months after my fourteenth birthday the first time it happened. I'd gone to bed around eleven and I was just about asleep when there was a light knock on the door. She came into my room and sat on the edge of my bed."

Madeline raised her head and my gaze darted quickly to her face. I could see the dawning horror in her eyes. The pain. Pain for me. She pressed her finger against my lips trying to halt my words.

"Nathaniel, you don't have to."

I kissed her fingertip before placing her hand back on my chest and covering it with mine. "It went on for almost a year. During that entire time I felt powerless. I didn't tell a single soul, not even my best friend. One night my dad came home unexpectedly after his business trip had been cut short. Denise started crying some sob story about how it was me who'd initiated the entire affair. I denied it, of course, but my father didn't believe me. He threw my clothes in a bag and tossed it outside onto the front yard, screaming at me to get out of his house. I knew nothing would change his mind, so I got dressed, grabbed my bag, and left. A year later my father tracked me down, begging me to forgive him. Apparently he'd discovered Denise attempting to seduce a neighbor kid and realized how wrong he'd been."

"Did you?" Madeline asked softly. "Forgive him, I mean?"

My voice was steely. "I punched him in the face, breaking his nose. Then I told him to go to hell. That was the last time I ever saw him. Shortly after that I went to college and got my Bachelor's and Master's in criminology. When I graduated, I went to work for the state corrections system before deciding I wanted to join the FBI. I wanted to be the kind of person who helped victims. It wasn't long before I grew jaded and cynical, mostly at the system. The injustices I've seen in my lifetime would haunt your dreams. Hell, sometimes they haunt mine."

Madeline caressed my cheek. "Have you had counseling? That's some heavy stuff to deal with. It really does help to have someone to talk to. I'm not just saying that because of my job either."

I shrugged. "I passed the psych eval. That's all I care about. Honestly, I enjoy the darkness inside. It's been a part of me so long, it's like a long-lost friend. I'd be an entirely different person without it."

Her lips drew down into a frown and I knew she wanted to say more on the topic, but she resisted. Instead she asked a different question. "How did Joseph make his way past your defenses?"

"With my charming wit and personality."

I merely chuckled while Madeline whipped her head around with a startled noise at Joseph's interruption.

"You scared the crap out of me," she scolded him.

He smiled a little too innocently as he strode into the room and set his computer bag on the floor next to the coffee table. Then he collapsed, exhaustion evident in his entire body, into the recliner next to the couch where Madeline and I were sitting.

"Sounds like I walked in on a deep and interesting conversation. You're wanting to know how I weaseled my way into this a-hole's life? Pure determination I tell you. Our friend Nathaniel here was the meanest, most ornery motherfucker I'd ever met. Imagine my horror when we were assigned to work on a case together. He made my life hell, I tell you." Joseph let out an exaggerated sigh of despair.

"You were a wet-behind-the-ears rookie I got stuck with. I was the one who was dying. Slowly and painfully. You were like this goofy puppy who excitedly pissed everywhere. Annoying little shit."

He flipped me off. "I was annoying right up until the moment you got shot."

Madeline gasped, her eyes tracking my chest searching for a bullet hole.

"Back shot. We were making an arrest on a member of the Gambino family when the man's wife pulled out a damn gun. I remember the sound of gunfire followed by excruciating pain and hearing Joseph yelling my name, but after that, it's all a blur. This time I truly was dying slowly and painfully. Next thing I know, I'm waking up in a hospital room with tubes and wires coming out of my entire body and this guy"—I jerked my chin in Joseph's direction—"asleep in the recliner on the other side of the room."

"We've been best friends ever since." Joseph replied smugly. "Probably because I'm the only one who puts up with his crabby ass."

CHAPTER 19

$\mathcal{M}$adeline

I LOVED WATCHING THE BANTER BETWEEN THE TWO OF THEM. THERE was so much brotherly love and trust there. In the back of my mind, I'd been waiting for signs of jealousy or hints that a ménage relationship wasn't really what they wanted. But seeing their ease with each other and how they treated me made me realize that this was real. Nathaniel was right. Vince and I just hadn't fit together. There wasn't anything wrong with either of us. It was just that the pieces of us that were needed to feel whole didn't match up. I wasn't the right sub for Vince and he wasn't the right Dom for me. Instead of feeling sad about it, I was actually happy, because it led me to Joseph and Nathaniel. I'd fallen hard for them.

Not even thinking about what I was doing, I moved from Nathaniel's lap. I took off my glasses and leaned over to set them on the end table, then shrugged out of my robe and tossed it on the floor next to the couch. I pulled my tank over my head, dropped it, slid my boy shorts down my legs, and stepped out of them. Nathaniel sucked in a breath and his gaze roamed appreciatively over my naked flesh. I returned to his lap, this time to straddle it. I pulled my hair over my shoulder and leaned down to press my mouth to his. I knew he was letting me lead at the moment, but ultimately he was still in control.

His mouth parted beneath mine, and my tongue darted in. His fingers gripped my hips tightly when I rocked my core against his erection. We kissed for a long moment before I pulled back. I looked over at Joseph who remained patiently sitting in the chair. I crooked my finger, beckoning him over to join us. He didn't hesitate. I continued rocking my pelvis against Nathaniel's even as the heat of Joseph's chest soaked into my back. Strong hands wrapped around my breasts, molding them. I covered the rough hands with my own, my head falling back against his shoulder.

"I want to take you bare," Nathaniel murmured against my lips. "We're tested yearly at work and it's been months since we've been with anyone."

The thought of his seed filling me sent an exhilarated thrill through my body. "Yes."

"Lift up," he growled.

I raised up slightly and a zipper sounded. When I lowered myself, I sighed in pleasure as his cock entered my pussy. I ground myself against him, forcing him even deeper. I knew I'd have bruises on my hips from the strength of his grip. He thrust upward hitting that spot inside me, and I almost came right there.

Joseph continued his sensual touch to my breasts, pinching and plucking at my nipples sending a shooting sensation of pleasure straight to where Nathaniel and I were connected. One of his hands left my breast and glided upward to my throat, his fingers encircling it. I froze.

"Do you trust me, angel?" he rasped softly in my ear.

I swallowed hard. "Yes, Master," I whispered back.

"Good. Nat's going to fuck you hard now. Are you ready?"

"Yes, Master," I repeated, swallowing one more time as I felt Joseph's other arm wrap around my waist and pull me tight against his chest.

Then, Nathaniel began to move. His thrusts were controlled. He began shallow at first while Joseph's hold on my throat tightened by minuscule amounts. I could still draw breath, but my inhalations were shallow. He was careful where he pressed and how hard. My heart beat out of control knowing what he was going to do. Sensation after sensation flowed through me. My head was buzzing and the tension in my core was spreading. My pussy throbbed.

Harder and harder Nathaniel pounded into me going deeper with each thrust. He angled his hips so he hit a different spot inside me every time. The faster he moved, the tighter Joseph's hold on my neck got. I was seeing every color of the rainbow, and it was beautiful. Suddenly the colors exploded and I gasped in air, sucking in deep breaths, pulling oxygen back into my lungs as the most powerful orgasm ever crashed over me.

Nathaniel roared beneath me and spilled his seed. I collapsed backward, Joseph catching me in his arms. He pulled me off Nathaniel's lap and cradled me against his chest. He moved to the couch and sat beside his partner, who placed my feet across his lap and rested his arms across the top of my legs. I laid there, exhausted, breathing in the scent of my two men and sex. I was utterly spent.

"Thank you for trusting me, Madeline."

I glanced up at Joseph and swore I saw love beaming from his eyes. I wondered what he saw reflecting back from mine.

"There's no one in the world I trust more than the two of you."

For the longest time, the three of us remained together. We didn't speak, perhaps in order to not disturb the bond we'd just built. The ringing of the phone broke the silence, and I wanted to throw it across the room.

Nathaniel gently pried my legs off him and rose from the

couch to snatch up the offending piece of technology. I almost felt sorry for whoever was on the other end of the line. Almost. While he spoke to the caller I stayed where I was since Joseph didn't appear in any hurry to move. Within moments, Nathaniel returned, his countenance even darker than usual.

"There's been a possible lead in the sex trafficking case. Reynolds wants us in the office stat."

I felt Joseph's sigh.

"Sorry, angel, we have to go." He stood, pulling me up with him.

"I understand. Go. Take care of whatever it is you need to. We'll talk when you get home."

He looked like he wanted to say something more, but instead gave me a kiss before disappearing up the stairs to get ready. Nat followed suit. I sank back onto the couch, oblivious to my own nakedness and thought about what I wanted to say when I saw them again tonight.

"...and, if God choose, I shall but love thee better after death."
- Elizabeth Barrett Browning, Sonnet 43

My dearest Madeline,

It feels as though a lifetime has passed since I first fell in love with you. I believed you to be perfect. Perfect for me. Your spirit called to me on a visceral level. Every time I saw you, your smile would light up the room. Your eyes sparkled like the sun's reflection on fresh, white snow. The glittering, natural diamond that Mother Nature carefully crafted. Its beauty unmatched. Until you. Your beauty outshone the brightest gem. But even gems become tarnished. Dirty. Like you. For so long I waited for you to realize we were meant to be together. For you to finally see me.

Instead, I discover you're nothing but a whore. A filthy whore who has let not just one man, but two, defile her. I've seen you three together you know. Entering Satan's den. You thought you could hide your perversion and sin behind closed doors, but you can't hide from me. I see you, Madeline. I've always seen you. Even when you didn't know I was watching. I thought you were different. The one. For over twenty years I've been waiting for you. But now, it's come to this.

It's time. Time to collect the heart that belongs to me. Has always belonged to me. And when your heart is in my possession, it will finally beat. For me. As it was meant to. Then we can be together. Forever.

CHAPTER 20

$\mathcal{M}$adeline

AFTER THE MEN LEFT, I'D QUICKLY SHOWERED AND GOT READY FOR work. I planned on stopping at my favorite bakery, *Jane Doughs*, before heading to my office. They'd just introduced a new chocolate and orange scone, and I was dying to try it. I wasn't afraid to admit chocolate was my weakness. Add in orange and I was in heaven times two. Before I'd starting staying at Joseph and Nathaniel's two weeks before, I'd always driven to my office since it had only been about twenty minutes from my home in Cherrydale to my office in Tenleytown. However, with D.C. traffic, and traveling to and from Maryland now, that wasn't a feasible option at the moment. I'd be commuting for hours each day.

So, we took the Metro instead. It had taken me a week to get used to public transportation and navigating the rail system. We didn't have that where I'd lived in North Carolina. Nathaniel, Joseph, and I walked the short distance to the Metro stop near their house and took the train into the city. We got off near FBI headquarters and then they walked me to my next stop at the Chinatown Station. From there my shadows took over and escorted me to Tenleytown. Luckily, my office building was only a short walk from the Metro stop.

"Morning, Madeline," Jane, the owner, hollered out when the bell signaled my entrance. I stepped inside, the scent of yeast and sweetness filling my nose. It smelled delicious, and my mouth began to water.

"Hey there. I hope you saved me one of those special chocolate and orange scones you've been teasing me about for over a week now," I tossed back, setting my briefcase on the counter and hopping up onto the bar stool, smoothing my skirt over my knees.

Jane merely laughed. "Of course I did. I knew you'd never stop harassing me if I didn't. Give me just a sec and I'll bring it right out."

My eyes scanned the brightly lit shop with its festive colors of pink, teal, and yellow. It was adorably decorated, warm and inviting, and made you feel like you were in someone's home. There was a small crowd inside, some of them business people clearly on their way to work. Just then, Jane came from around the display case, a teal dessert plate in hand. There, taking up almost the entire plate was the most mouth-watering scone I think I'd ever laid eyes on. I rolled my eyes in ecstasy and I hadn't even taken my first bite yet. It didn't matter. I knew it was going to rock my world. She set the plate in front of me with a flourish.

"Bon appétit."

"Merci." I dipped my head in thanks.

"You're welcome. Sorry, that's all the French I know," she shrugged.

I laughed. "Hey, you know more than me."

While I took a bite of my pastry, Jane stood there, waiting for my verdict. Holy shit, the damn thing was practically melting in

125

my mouth. I savored that single bite while she smiled at me, her expression knowing.

"Oh my God, this is the most amazing thing ever! Are you sure I can't steal you away so you can become my own personal pastry chef?"

"You wouldn't be the first person to offer that position to me. Sadly, I'll have to decline."

"Damn. Well, at least I tried. Thank you so much for bringing this deliciousness into my world. You go back to your customers and I'm gonna sit here and enjoy this masterpiece you've created."

Jane blushed and waved her towel at me as she hustled to greet a new customer at the counter. In the meantime, I took tiny bites of my treat, trying to make it last. I didn't want to be done with it. While I sat there, my eyes wandered around the room again. I caught a man with salt and pepper hair, around my age, sitting alone at a table on the far wall staring at me. I gave a brief, polite smile before looking away. Something about the way he looked at me had me on edge. I hurriedly took the last few bites of the pastry, suddenly wanting to leave.

I rifled through my briefcase and tossed a few bills on the counter before briskly walking outside. I heard Jane call out to me, but I ignored her. I'd have to apologize later. My gut told me to get away. I didn't look back, but I prayed my two shadows stayed close. I practically ran the three blocks to my office building. When I arrived I was breathless. Then, I felt like an idiot for acting like such a scaredy cat. The man had done nothing untoward. He hadn't appeared menacing in any way. Still, something about the way he'd looked at me gave me the creeps. A chill crawled across my neck. Within a few hours of seeing clients though, I'd completely forgotten the man from the bakery.

~

"TODAY WAS A GREAT SESSION, PETER, AND WE COVERED A LOT OF

ground. Next week, I see a huge breakthrough coming. Just keep journaling and remember your breathing techniques, okay?"

The shy young man nodded. "Yes ma'am. I'll see you next week, Doc. Thanks for everything."

"You're more than welcome. Have a great weekend." I waved as he closed the waiting room door behind him.

Sighing, I turned and headed back to my office to finish up a last bit of paperwork. My head was starting to ache and I was ready to go home. I paused at the thought. Since when had I started thinking of Nathaniel and Joseph's place as *home*? The more I thought about it though, the more it rang true. It wasn't the townhouse though. It was them. *They* were home. My Doms. With that final realization my heart unlocked and there was a shift inside me. They'd both shown me that we belonged together, the three of us, but I'd continued to keep a section of my heart hidden. Out of fear. My entire life, every thing that seemed too good to be true always turned out that way. This time that wasn't the case. Happiness welled up inside and poured out of me. I shoved my chair back, and threw out my arms, spinning around, giggling with excitement like a little girl.

"Hello, Madeline."

I screeched at the baritone greeting and threw my foot down to stop the momentum of my chair, my head whipping around to face the owner of the voice. In the doorway of my office was a non-nondescript, slender man with salt and pepper hair and a crooked smile on his face. It took me only a second, but a single blink later, I recognized him. My heart stopped beating for a blip in time and then suddenly, it was racing and that sinking feeling of dread in my gut returned. It hit me at that moment what he'd said. I remained in my chair, tense but alert, trying not to panic. My voice came out steadier than I expected. "I'm sorry, but the office is closed for the day. I'm not taking any new patients at this time."

The man stepped inside my office, slowly, his hands in his

pockets as though he didn't have a care in the world. As though he hadn't just intruded in my place of work. He strolled further in, confident, like he owned the place, his eerie gaze never leaving me. There wasn't a hint of warmth in his blue eyes. They were empty.

Soulless.

Evil.

He cocked his head inquisitively; his emotionless, icy gaze homed in on me. A sinister smile flickered across his lips before smoothing out again.

"I think you need to leave," I stood from my chair and made to move toward the door when he remained silent.

"For years I've looked for you. Every time I thought I found you, it turned out to be the wrong woman. Do you know how frustrating it is to think you've located the love of your life, only to discover she's a stranger?"

Who the hell was this guy?

Steadily I crept closer to the door, keeping a close eye on him, watching, waiting for any signs of movement. "I'm sorry, but I think you have me confused with someone else, sir."

He sneered, ugliness now marring his expression. "Don't tell me what I think, Madeline," he spat.

I threw my hands up in a placating manner, trying not to notice how they shook and trembled. "I apologize. I can understand your frustration. I would feel the same way if the person I loved didn't return my love."

The man took a step in my direction and I froze.

"When you got my first letter, I waited for you," he continued as though I'd never spoken. "For days I waited for you in our special place, but you never came. With every letter I sent, I kept hoping you'd understand what I tried telling you. Instead, I was left with bitter disappointment."

He took another step, but this time it brought him to the chair reserved for my patients. I tried to understand and piece together what he was saying, but nothing he said made sense. He took a seat and crossed one ankle over his knee. He leaned back, facing me, and threaded his fingers together to lay over his stomach. His eyes never left mine, and even though he was no longer standing, I was still afraid to take another step. He remained watchful.

My men were supposed to be picking me up from work. I just needed to stall until they arrived. I also wanted answers, so for the moment I needed to play along so I tried to appear contrite. "I'm sorry I didn't come. That I didn't understand what you were trying to tell me."

With my apology, finally, some emotion flickered across his face. It looked like hope, but it was quickly erased. "I sent you clue after clue and still you remained oblivious. Then, I realized you had forgotten. About me. About us."

I could see his muscles shifting, tightening, then loosening. His jaw clenched and unclenched like he was trying to control his emotions. His gaze shifted and became unfocused, like he became lost in some memory. I didn't hesitate. Instead, I raced out my office and through the waiting room. My scream echoed in the air, before being abruptly extinguished by a large, calloused hand slamming over my mouth. Another hand wrapped around my waist, trapping my arms at my side, and he ripped me backwards trapping me against his body. I thrashed and kicked as muffled cries tried to escape, but the strength of his hand held them, and me, back.

I tried to stomp on his foot, but he anticipated the move and wrapped his leg around my hip and knee to block my movement. The force knocked us off balance and we fell forward. I landed face first against the waiting room couch, the cushions softening my landing. Instantly, he jerked me back to my feet and threw me forward again, his hold never loosening. I screamed in pain when the side of my head bashed into the wall. Dizzy with a possible concussion, the fight in me slowed. Pounding pain filled my head and my ears rang.

With my body caught between the wall and the surprisingly powerful stranger behind me, I was helpless, immobile. Tears and snot clogged my nose and I began to panic, afraid I was going to suffocate. My brain screamed to fight, to get free, but there was no room for me to move. *Please, I don't want to die,* I silently begged. *Not now when I'd just found love. The missing pieces of my soul. God—someone—please help me.*

The room rushed past me as he spun me around, the hand leaving my mouth, before instantly slamming back against it, effectively silencing me again. I hissed at the sharp pain in my neck. A flash of silver caught my eye and my gaze zoomed in on the knife being waved in front of me, a drop of blood on its tip. My eyes widened and I inhaled, not getting nearly enough air through my nose. I was starting to feel lightheaded and my vision was dimming around the edges.

"Don't move. Don't scream. Do you understand?" The instructions were delivered calmly, with no hint of breathlessness in its delivery, despite the resistance I'd demonstrated.

Frantically, I nodded in agreement. The hand over my face loosened and pulled away. I gasped in deep, cleansing breaths, desperate to fill my lungs. I forced myself to slow my breathing for fear of hyperventilating. The man, Casanova I assumed, shifted his body slightly away from mine, but the knife remained near my throat.

"Please"—I tearfully choked out—"please don't kill me. I'll do whatever you want."

He slammed his fist into the wall beside my head, spittle spewing out of his mouth and all over my face. I didn't dare wipe it away. "I just want you to love me like I love you!"

"I ca—I can do that," I stuttered, willing to agree to anything if only he'd let me go.

He stepped back, taking the knife with him. "Oh, I know you can. I'll make you."

My abuser snatched me by the hair and yanked me away from

the wall. I screeched and stumbled at the force, but managed to stay on my feet.

"You're coming with me. We're gonna walk down the hall to the fire escape outside the window. From there, we're climbing down and you're going to get in the van at the bottom. I'll be in front of you the whole time. Don't attempt to escape or call for help in anyway or I'll kill you. Do you understand?"

I winced when he pulled my hair again, but ground out, "Yes, I understand."

"Good. Now let's go."

He pushed me out the door and toward the end of the hall all while I prayed for Nathaniel and Joseph to find me.

CHAPTER 21

oseph

"THIS COLLAR IS BURNING A HOLE IN MY POCKET."

Nat was friends with a Dom whose submissive crafted stunning, one-of-a-kind collars and sold them online. A week ago we'd made an appointment with her to discuss designing one for Madeline. I'd picked it up today. We weren't planning on presenting it to her immediately, but one day soon she was going to wear it. There wasn't a doubt in my mind. She was the one for us. I knew she continued to hold back a piece of herself, but we were patient men. Well, I was anyway, although Nat was learning.

Madeline had changed him. Gone was the angry man walking around with the weight of the world balanced on his shoulders. He was learning to cope with the fact that bad shit happened, and he couldn't always save everyone. It was a weary weight he carried, but Madeline was making him realize that he didn't have to carry it alone.

"She's not quite ready for it yet. Almost. Just not yet."

My eyes widened in mock surprise. "Did I hear you right? Is this the same man who bulldozed his way into a private meeting between the Assistant Director and the Deputy Director, because he was tired of waiting out in the hall?"

Nat shot me the finger as we waited for the elevator in the lobby of the office building where Madeline practiced on the fifth floor. "Fuck off, Crocker," he cursed good-naturedly, making me laugh. "I'm working on my patience. For Madeline."

The elevator dinged and its doors opened. I stepped in behind him and pressed the button for Madeline's floor. "You're doing surprisingly well if I'm being honest. I never thought I'd see the day when we'd find the right submissive to mellow even your temper."

Nat's grin flattened and his expression turned serious. "I'm at peace when I'm near her. All the chaos around me disappears and I can just... be."

The bell dinged for her floor and I smacked him lightly on the shoulder before giving it a light squeeze. "I know the feeling, man."

We stepped out of the elevator and headed toward Madeline's office midway down the hall. *That's weird.* My steps sped up when I noticed the waiting room door open. It was always shut when we got here. Nat followed suit.

"Fuck," he shouted, both of us whipping out our sidearms when we saw the condition of the room. Magazines lay scattered everywhere and the couch cushions were half falling on the floor. With our guns at ready, we swept the room.

"Madeline?" I called out, even though I knew she wasn't going to answer. "God damn it."

The waiting area was clear, her office the same. Nat holstered his weapon when I gave the all clear.

"Get on the phone now and get me those surveillance videos," I directed as I returned to the hallway to scan for any other signs. I swept my weapon from side to side, pausing at each door I passed while I scanned the hallway. I paused for a moment at something on the wall. *Son of a bitch.* It looked like blood, but the forensic team would need to make a positive ID.

Nat appeared at my side. "The ERT is on their way. IT is working on getting the feed, but they said they're having a challenge. It looks like there was a jam in the signal. They're doing the best they can. Is that blood?" There was a hint of panic in his question. Something I couldn't remember ever hearing from him.

"It looks like it, but that doesn't mean it's hers, Nat."

"We can't lose her."

"We won't. That's a promise. Right now we need to focus on keeping our shit together. We need to treat this like any other case. Let the team process the scene and use what they find, which means we wait for them to get here."

FORTY AGONIZING MINUTES LATER, THE SAME ERT AND IT TEAM that had processed Madeline's house arrived. While we waited for them, we'd run down to the lobby where Agents Campbell and Evans were stationed. I was pissed at myself for not forcing the issue when Madeline wanted them to remain in the lobby, saying that they would intimidate her patients. None of us thought Casanova would make his move in such a public place. I took full responsibility for this happening. I'd never forgive myself if something happened to her. Unfortunately, neither Campbell nor Evans could give us any information. We instructed them to remain until the two teams left in case we needed them for something.

The ERT began the arduous task of dusting for fingerprints, taking the scrapings of what we thought was blood off the wall, as well as packaging strands of hair. They were painstakingly thorough in their task. It was taking forever, but I didn't complain because the more diligent they were in gathering the evidence, the better chance we had of finding Madeline. The IT guys, on the other hand, were running into more challenges.

Kurt's fingers were flying across his keyboard, his eyes darting back and forth on his screen trying to make sense of the scrambled feed he kept getting. "Damn, this guy is good. He knows his stuff that's for sure. Every program I run is coming up against a roadblock. This is going to take some time. However, I think I got a hit on a surveillance video across the street. This convenience store has been robbed several times so a couple weeks ago they installed some extra cameras. One of them points directly at this building. They're new enough that I don't think anyone even realized they were put in."

Trying not to get my hopes up, I stood behind Kurt as he pulled up a video feed. I checked the time stamp and it was just past sixteen hundred thirty hours. Nat's focus was on the same screen as we watched people entering and exiting the office building. The picture was grainy due to the low quality camera, but it was better than nothing.

"Wait, go back. Look, there, in the alley." Nat pointed a finger at a small area on the right side of the screen. Kurt clicked a few buttons and the video rewound before another click of a button had the video playing again. I homed in on the area he was directing us to.

"Stop."

The frame froze on the screen.

"Can you zoom in or pixelate that thing?"

Kurt glanced at Nat. "Pixelate?"

"Whatever you call it when you make a blurry image clear by upping the resolution."

Silence spread throughout the room. Nat took his eyes off the screen to see why no one was moving only to find Kurt and me staring at him. Me in surprise, Kurt seemingly impressed. Nat only shrugged.

"What? Sometimes I pay attention to what the fuck you egg heads are doing. Either way, can you do it?"

Kurt turned back to the computer and rat-tat-tatted away at the keys. "Of course I can do it. I just needed a moment to start my heart back up."

"Fuck off," Nat threw back heatedly. He was anxious to find her. Our world would cave in if something happened to her.

The three of us concentrated on the screen, tension and impatience thick in the air with the wait to see what showed up. Slowly, the image on the screen shifted and started to become less blurry until finally a clearer picture stared back at us. Fuck, that was Madeline. Who was the man with her?

Obviously anticipating our next command, Kurt beat us to it. "Running facial recognition next. It's going to be tough though. The entirety of the man's face isn't in view. Which means I'm going to have to recreate his image and then run it through and hope for a hit. There's no guarantees. And it's going to take me a while, maybe a couple hours. I have to run back to the lab for my computer there. I don't have the capabilities I need while mobile."

"Do what you have to do as quickly as possible. Send me that shot as well. I want to show it to the security team that's been shadowing Madeline. See if they recognize him."

Kurt closed his laptop and hastily gathered up his stuff. "You got it. I'll give you a call if and when I find something."

Grudgingly accepting there was nothing more we could do here, we knew our only options were to wait for the ERT to take the evidence back to headquarters and begin examining it. In the meantime, I was heading downstairs to talk with Campbell and Evans again.

CHAPTER 22

$\mathcal{M}$adeline

My shoulders and arms screamed in agony from being tied too tightly behind my back, and I was pretty sure my wrists were bleeding. I'd been bound during rope play and bondage scenes, but the Dom always played safe. This psychopath was definitely not playing safe. My fingers had gone numb long ago, and I was starting to get a cramp in my left shoulder from my awkward side-lying position.

Once we'd made it to the van, my captor had thrown me in the back, leapt in after me, and slammed the door behind us. He'd tied my hands, jerking on the zip ties. My neck continued to sting where he'd cut me. Not one single pain was worse than the other. My entire body hurt. But I was alive. I had to keep reminding myself of that fact. As long as I stayed alive, there was a chance that Nathaniel and Joseph would find me. I held onto that thought, like someone holding on to that last grain of sand in an hourglass.

I'd tried to sit up when we'd first begun moving, but a barked command to remain where I was kept me frozen. I switched to asking questions, but gave up when the only thing I got in return was silence. Every bump sent shards of pain through me. I had no idea how long we'd been driving, but the raging silence was making me go out of my mind. The silence was a total mind fuck, and if that was his intent then he was doing a fantastic job.

Under a darkening sky, the van slowed. The only thing I could see through the windshield was the red, gold, oranges, and yellows of the trees above us. We could have been traveling one hour or three and we could have been anywhere. I had no idea. I'd lost all track of time and direction while I attempted to puzzle out who the hell this man was. My abductor continued driving slowly, my body shifting slightly as the van made several turns. Eventually, it came to a complete stop. The front door opened and closed. My head swiveled around trying to figure out what door was going to open next. Nothing.

The sky grew darker and I remained alone. I was terrified of even moving. My primary goal was to remain alive until my men arrived. I'd do whatever I had to in order to make that happen. I was a psychologist. My goal was to get my patients talking. That's what I needed to do. Although, if the drive to wherever we were was any indication, getting him to talk may prove more of a challenge than I thought. Suddenly, the back door of the van opened.

"Let's go."

The man stepped to the side, leaning against the door, and motioned with his hand for me to move. Apparently that was the only help I was going to get. I shimmied and squirmed and pulled myself forward until I reached the end of the vehicle. Unfolding my legs, I leaned forward until they reached the ground and stood. I hissed in pain when he snatched me by my arm.

"Please, untie me, or at least loosen my bindings. I can't feel my fingers, and I'm pretty sure I'm bleeding." My voice didn't quiver or waver. No matter how terrified I was, I had to force myself to remain calm.

His grip tightened in warning. "Don't make me repeat myself, Madeline."

Temporarily giving up the battle, I followed his lead, holding back my groan of pain when he jerked my arm again. I didn't want to give this piece of shit the satisfaction of knowing he was hurting me.

Now that I was outside, I was able to take in my surroundings, searching for any clues to our whereabouts. I needed to see what my options were. All around us were trees in full fall foliage. Trees so close to each other their branches and leaves intertwined like lovers. Nestled between small copses of trees was a small log cabin with a rickety front porch made up of warped slats of wood. The front windows were grimy and mud-covered. The steps were long worn out and replaced by cinder blocks.

The interior of the cabin was in sharp contrast to the run down exterior. Standing inside, it was like I'd been transported into a photoshoot straight out of *Log Cabin Living* magazine. It was completely modernized and new with bright lights shining out of the luminous chandelier hanging from the middle of the vaulted ceiling. There was an entire wall made of stone with a built-in fireplace, and the other wall nearest it was made of nothing but large windows. Between the lights being on and the darkness outside, I couldn't tell what the view outside the windows was. It contained an open floor concept where the kitchen, with its stainless steel appliances, bled into the living room.

"Turn around," he gruffly commanded.

I hesitated too long because he whipped out the knife and spun me around. I cried out, but slammed my mouth shut, cutting off further noise. Then I waited for the excruciating pain of the blade. Instead, he merely cut the zip ties off me. I hissed when he nicked my skin and my fingers screamed in agony as the blood finally began to flow again, the pins and needles sensation causing tears to form. Hoping there was still a reprieve from death, I turned to face my abductor, trying to rub my hands together to bring back feeling, but that only made it hurt worse, so I hung my arms at my sides and hoped it returned quickly.

"Thank you for untying me." I tried to remain courteous and not piss him off any further. His fuse was already short enough. And I still didn't know who the fuck he was.

He gestured to the cream colored couch with the knife. "Have a seat."

I followed his instruction without hesitation, the words *stay alive* playing on repeat in my head. No matter what he did to me, I only needed to stay alive. It was time to put my skills to use.

"You said I didn't even remember who you were. All I can say is I'm sorry for that. I've met so many people that sometimes I forget I've met someone. Sadly, I've always been better at names than faces. It's wholly unintentional, but I know it's a flaw I have." I kept my voice soft and coaxing like I was speaking to one of my nervous patients.

He stared at me like he was trying to gauge my sincerity. Whatever he saw must have appeased him, because he gave a small smile and shook his head like I was a silly child. He positioned himself in the adjacent chair, ankle crossed over one knee, and leaned back with both arms splayed over the armrests in a completely relaxed position, if you ignored the knife still clasped in his hand. Unlike me, who sat ramrod straight, tense, and ready to bolt if given the opportunity.

"You always did know how to make things better. Like that time when Billy Pritchard threw a rock at me during recess." His eyes took on a glassy and unfocused glaze that spoke of getting lost in the memory.

I kept my mouth shut and let him continue.

"I remember you walking right over to Billy and kicking him

in the shin. You didn't say anything to me, but when we got in line to go back inside, you smiled at me. It was like we shared a secret."

My mind raced with the information. I vaguely recalled a boy in my class named Billy when I was in sixth grade, but God, that was a lifetime ago. Almost thirty years. I certainly had no recollection of kicking him in the shin for any offense or another. The man across from me refocused his gaze and glanced over at me. There was such a look of longing and hope in his eyes, like he idolized me even after all these years. I didn't know what to say, so I improvised. "Billy always was a jerk."

My captor's eyes danced with delight at my insult and he chuckled. "That's why I killed him."

"Excuse me?" The horrified question slipped out before I could stop it.

The man shrugged. "I hated that smug shithead. He always thought he was better than everyone. I tracked him down a few years ago, and when the time was right, I took my knife to him. Pissed himself, the pussy. He always acted like he was some tough guy, but man, when I slid my blade into him? He sure wasn't so cocky then. Cried like a fucking baby." He brought the knife up to his lips and tapped it on lips that lifted into a smile while he appeared to lose himself again in the recollection.

Jesus, this guy was a fucking psychopath. He murdered without conscience. I wondered how many people were dead because of him.

"Was he the first person you killed?" I asked, morbidly curious.

CHAPTER 23

athaniel

JOSEPH AND I WERE HALFWAY DOWN TO THE LOBBY WHEN OUR phones pinged signaling an incoming email. I pulled it up and saw it was from Kurt. Damn that guy worked fast. Our gazes zeroed in on the two-man team waiting for us in the lobby.

"Campbell. Evans."

They scrambled from their positions and hurried over.

"Do you recognize this guy?" I turned my phone toward them with the snapshot of Madeline and the guy in the alley.

Evans shook his head, while Campbell studied it a bit longer. "Wasn't he the guy at the bakery this morning? I mean, I'm not a hundred percent sure, but it could be him."

"What bakery?" Joseph asked.

Campbell spoke again. "Ms. Parrish stopped at her favorite bakery this morning. She's usually there at least twice a week. She's friends with the owner. Anyway, we stopped there this morning. I'm great with faces, and I'm always watching the crowd.

There was a guy in there this morning that resembles your guy here. It's hard to make a guaranteed assumption though with only a partial of his face."

"You know, Ms. Parrish did rush out of the bakery pretty quickly. Almost like she was spooked about something. Nothing seemed out of the ordinary so I didn't really think anything on it," Evans tacked on, shaking his head. "Damn, I should have paid more attention."

"You talking about *Jane Doughs?*"

They both nodded. "Yes, sir."

"You two report back to headquarters. I want you to head to evidence and see what the ERT has come up with. Call us immediately if they get a hit on anything. Joseph, let's go."

We ran out to the car and raced the few blocks to the bakery, praying it was still open. When we pulled up, Joseph cursed. "Son of a bitch."

"Let's knock on the door. Maybe someone is still in the back."

I pounded on the door praying all the while. Then, we waited. Nothing. I pounded again. *God damnit.*

"Look, I'll put in a call and search the owner's information to get a number."

We turned and headed back to the car. Just as I stepped off the curb to walk around to the driver's side, the sound of a bell jingled.

"Can I help you?"

We both turned at the melodic voice. A petite woman with reddish-blonde hair piled on top of her head stood holding the door of the bakery open. She had a heart-shaped face with that girl-next-door look and appeared to be in her late-twenties or early-thirties.

"Are you Jane?" I asked, hopeful that this was the woman we needed to speak with.

"Yes. Can I help you?" she asked cautiously, unsure of our intent.

143

I sighed in relief and my shoulders relaxed from their tensed position as I reached into my pocket for my ID. "My name is Agent Nathaniel Morgan and this is Agent Joseph Crocker. We need—"

"Wait a minute. Are you *the* Nathaniel and Joseph? Like Madeline's Nathaniel and Joseph?"

Joseph and I looked at each other in surprise and then back at Jane. "She's told you about us?"

Her face flushed a light pink shade and she lowered her gaze before returning it back. "Um, she may have mentioned something."

I knew Joseph felt the same rush of pride that Madeline had told her friend about us. It also looked like there was also a hint of envy in little miss Jane's tone.

"Jane, we need your help. Madeline has gone missing, we believe kidnapped. We know she was in here this morning. And that it's possible something spooked her. You don't happen to have any cameras in there do you?" I gestured toward the shop.

Her eyes widened in horror. "Oh my God. Yes, of course. Come in. I'll pull the tapes for you."

We entered the bakery and Jane closed and locked the door behind us. "The camera monitor is back here."

She led us through the saloon-style swinging door into the back, around racks of covered baked goods, until we reached a small office. Jane took a seat in the office chair and tapped the keyboard.

"Sorry, I have such ancient equipment. My father owned the bakery before me and still lived in archaic times when it comes to technology. It's just something I haven't gotten around to upgrading yet."

I shook off her apologies. "Don't worry about it."

"If you give me just a second, I can rewind the tapes all the way back to this morning when Madeline arrived."

"Actually, can you go back further than that? We're looking for a guy that might have already been here waiting."

She shot us a questioning glance, but did as we asked. "I'll roll back to when we opened."

I nodded my thanks. The three of us stared at the monitor, watching the fast moving images on the screen play backwards. I thought I caught a glimpse of Madeline in one frame, but it went by too quickly. A few moments later, the image blacked out. There was some brief static and then the picture cleared. We watched as customers came and left with still no sign of our potential suspect.

"Is there any way to speed up the frames without specifically fast-forwarding?" I asked after twenty minutes of absolutely nothing. We'd be here all day at this rate, and we didn't have that kind of time.

Jane bit her lip in uncertainty. "Maybe. Let me try something."

She fiddled with a couple buttons and soon the frames began progressing faster, but not so fast that we couldn't see every detail. Frame after frame passed quickly, but still nothing. It was closing in on the time that Madeline had arrived and I'd just about given up any hope that this was going to lead us to someone. That was until we got to the 7:32 a.m. time stamp.

"Shit, there. Slow it back down, please." Joseph and I sat up, alert now that a new customer had walked into the bakery. The screen speed slowed and we watched as a man whose entire face wasn't visible yet stood at the counter ordering. He turned as though to look over his shoulder toward the door and his entire face came into view.

"Him," Joseph pointed to the man now visible. "Do you recognize that guy?"

Jane leaned forward to stare closely at the screen, studying it with narrowed eyes. "Yeah, his name is Grady. He's been a regular for the last month or so. Comes in a few times a week, always sits at the same table. Nice guy, tips well."

"Do you know Grady's last name?" I couldn't keep the

excitement out of my voice that maybe we were going to get this guy.

She shook her head. "No, I'm sorry I don't. He's never told me, and I've never asked."

"Does he ever pay with a credit card? Maybe this morning? Would you have a receipt, anything, with his full name on it?"

Her shoulders fell. "He always pays cash to my knowledge."

"Fuck," Joseph jumped from his chair and began to pace, his fingers laced behind his head.

"I wish I could help more."

I reached out and laid my hand on her forearm. "You've helped more than you know. Thank you."

It felt weird being the one offering comfort to someone. Usually that was Joseph's job. He was the one who was good at it. Me? I was usually the one cursing and pacing. I rose to take my place next to Joseph.

"Let's go talk to Kurt. Give him our guy's name and see what he can come up with."

Joseph stopped pacing to look over at me before nodding. I turned back to Jane.

"Can we take this tape with us?"

"Of course," she hurriedly removed the surveillance video before handing it to me.

I took it from her hands. "Thanks for your time. We really do appreciate it."

"I hope Madeline is alright. If I think of anything else, I promise to call you."

We weaved our way through the kitchen again and out through the bakery until we reached the car. I knew Joseph was hanging on by a thread. I knew, because I felt the exact same way.

"We'll find her."

There was no reply as I pulled away from the curb and headed back to FBI headquarters. We needed to meet with Kurt. I only prayed we weren't too late to save her.

CHAPTER 24

*M*adeline

"So, was he?" I asked again when Casanova didn't respond.

"No. My father was first."

"I see. What did your father do to deserve to die?"

He stared into the cold, empty fireplace, arms crossed defensively over his chest. "I don't want to talk about it."

"That's fine. You don't have to. But what about your mother? Is she still... around?" I needed to step lightly with my questioning, because I didn't want to ask anything that might set him off. Especially considering his response to my last question.

"My mother is still back in Mill Valley. Even after all these years, she never could bear to leave."

A cold chill raced across the back of my neck, and a sickening knot of dread grew in my belly.

"Mill Valley, California?" My voice squeaked with the question.

He looked at me questioningly. "Of course, that's where we

grew up. You said you remembered Billy. He went to school with us."

I scrambled to think. "That's right. I don't know where my mind is. Wow, that was a lifetime ago."

"Twenty-five years. But, I'll never forget that day when you kicked Billy. I was the new kid in school and didn't have any friends yet. That day meant everything to me." He chuckled. "I think that was the day my love for you began. Every time you smiled at me, I held it close to my heart. I loved that we shared something special between us. I knew what you were trying to tell me every time you looked my way. That you felt the same way I did. The flutters in my belly whenever you were near. That sense of giddy anticipation knowing I'd see you at school the next day. I was devastated when you moved away and didn't tell me where you were going. You almost broke my heart. But then I realized that you would have told me if you could. Your parents didn't give you any time. So, I waited patiently until I grew up and could start looking for you. It's taken me this entire time to find you. Now that I have, we can be together. Forever."

Holy shit. Pieces were finally falling into place. I recalled a boy. An outcast. One who was always nearby. Following my friends and me around. They'd wanted me to tell him to leave us alone, but other than being a little weird, he hadn't bothered me. He didn't try to invite himself into our circle. He was content to remain on the sidelines. But he never strayed far from us. From me. Was this actually him? Had he really been searching for me since fifth grade?

"Grady?" I asked, hesitantly, hoping, yet dreading, I was right.

His eyes widened and his mouth formed the shape of a smile, his lips widening slightly to show the whites of his teeth. I stared intently at his features, trying to bring back the memory of an eleven-year old boy I'd barely known for a year. "See, you do remember me. I knew you would."

"Of...of course I remember you," I stuttered. My brain began to filter through everything he'd told me about the letters he'd written. About leaving me clues. About our secret place. I had no idea what he was talking about.

"I'm sorry I was so angry with you earlier. That I hurt you. I just got a little out of control when I thought you had no idea who I was. That you'd forgotten me and how much we meant to each other. It made me so angry. I just reacted."

The words were right, but the tone wasn't sincere. It was like he was reciting them by rote. Like he knew what he was supposed to say, but didn't have the emotion to back up the words. His eyes were still black with evil. Either way, it didn't matter. I didn't believe a word he was saying, but he didn't need to know that. I'd play along so long as it kept me alive.

I nodded sympathetically. "I understand. Sometimes our emotions get the best of us. It's only natural. I'm sure that's what happened with those other women."

Grady's brows crinkled in puzzlement and his head drew back slightly. "What other women?"

Now it was my turn to be confused. "The ones you killed."

"I have no idea what you're talking about. I didn't kill any women."

"But—" I swallowed hard. "What about the body in my backyard? The letters? I mean you're Casanova. They said you've killed five women."

He jumped up from his seat in agitation causing me to scramble backwards across the couch. "Stop saying that!"

"I'm sorry," I held my hands out in a placating gesture.

Grady paced back and forth, the knife still in one of the hands he clasped his head in like he was holding off a headache. Or something else. My eyes tracked the path he wove, keeping a close watch on him. I noticed he was mumbling under his breath, talking to himself. I jerked in alarm when he stopped suddenly and spun around to face me.

"Who the hell is Casanova?" he snapped.

I unfurled myself from my protective position wondering how much I should share with him. It was obvious he truly didn't know. Maybe I could make this work in my favor. "The FBI are looking for a serial killer who sends love letters to the women he kills. They think you're him. And now that you have me, they won't stop until they find me. And you."

"No, no, no," he screeched, his composure utterly rattled while he continued to pace. "This can't be happening."

I grew worrisome when his movements grew more frenetic and he started mumbling to himself again. Grady was blatantly unstable and this news was setting him off to the millionth degree. I was terrified for the consequences of this development and needed to try and diffuse the situation. "Grady, listen to me. Everything is going to be fine. I'll make sure they know you didn't harm any of those other women. I'll tell them there is someone else out there. They'll believe me."

He whipped around to face me, his expression completely flat, his body movements no longer fidgeting and twitchy, but rather smooth and fluid. His mouth twitched and then turned up on one side into a smirk before he let out a single guffaw followed by another and another until he was laughing manically. Only there was no humor in it. It was pure evil. I shivered when his soulless gaze continued to bore into me. "I'll make sure they know you didn't harm any of those women," he mockingly repeated my words in a falsetto tone, his eyelashes fluttering furiously.

His tone deepened several octaves with his next words.

"God, you both are so pathetic. Grady is such a pussy. And you"—he chuckled—"I have no idea what the fuck he ever saw in you. He followed you around with those sad ass puppy dog eyes and you just ate that shit up like you were some fucking goodie two shoes doing him a favor by letting him sniff around you. For twenty-five years he's been tracking you down like some desperate fool. I've been trying to tell him you didn't give a shit about him, but he never listens to me. Never has. He still doesn't realize you couldn't care less about him. The only person you care about is yourself and those two Feds you're fucking."

No way. I narrowed my eyes. "Who are you?"

He gestured to himself in mock-innocence. "Who? Me? You mean I forgot to introduce myself? I hadn't realized. How rude of me. My name is Jordan. I'm one of Grady's alters. You know what that is, don't you, Madeline? I mean being the genius quack doctor you are, right?"

I ignored his dig at my profession. "Yes, I know what that is. How many of you are there?"

He merely smiled. "Wouldn't you like to know? Are you wondering if they're all like me? If they don't take shit from anyone? Or are they all scared and pathetic like Grady?"

"I'm just curious." I tried to play off my insatiable need to find something to bring either Grady back or, if there was one, another alter. Hopefully one not as psychotic as this one.

Jordan stepped toward me, flashing his insidious smile, the knife in his hand reflecting the firelight. "I think it's about time we show you the truth. What do you think, Doc?"

Oh my God.

CHAPTER 25

oseph

IT WAS LIKE OUR ROLES WERE SUDDENLY REVERSED. NAT WAS THE calm and collected one, whereas I was raging both inside and out. I was barking at every colleague to get them moving faster toward finding Madeline. It was almost ten, and she'd been missing for five hours. I knew there was no chance I'd be getting any sleep tonight, which meant that most likely no one else was going to be sleeping either. I knew Nat wouldn't. He'd be the next one in line behind me pushing these people to get us some answers.

Kurt had already volunteered to stay and work on the case, which was where we were headed now. Nat trailed behind me as we made our way to his office. He was located in the basement in the far corner. I had no idea why anyone would want to be that far removed from the rest of the staff and offices, but it obviously suited him fine.

"Tell me you have something, Kurt," I bit out the minute we entered his domain, bypassing any sort of greeting.

Kurt remained tapping away at his keyboard, not offended in the least by my brusque demand.

"I was able to tap into various street cams and video feeds throughout the city. I caught a few glimpses of your suspect driving a white van with the back windows painted over in white. I got a tag number, but the plates were stolen. The last known spotting was on I-275 heading west out of the city. Unfortunately, after that, I haven't been able to find him again. But, I'm still working on it and this one other thing."

My toe tapped in a staccato rhythm matching the sound of his fingers pecking away at the keys. With a final heavy tap with flourish, he mimicked a bomb exploding with his hands and fingers.

"Boom. I got it." He turned and faced Nat and me. "So, I got a call from the forensics team. They found a partial print inside the house from when the dead woman was found. It wasn't much, but somehow they got lucky and were able to find a match in the system. It belongs to one Grady Larson, age thirty-seven, born in San Francisco. Mother, alive. Father, deceased. There was actually an investigation into his death in fact. The wife called the police saying she believed their son, Grady, murdered him. He was questioned, but no concrete evidence was found linking him to the crime. The coroner ruled it an accident. The son moved away shortly after the investigation was over, but the mother still lives in Mill Valley, just outside San Francisco."

"Have you figured out if there's a connection between Madeline and this Grady?" Nat asked.

Kurt sent an annoyed glance, almost affronted that Nat would doubt his thoroughness. "Of course I did. Apparently, they were in the same fifth grade class at Mill Valley North. The Larson's had just moved to town and the younger Larson began attending a new school. Your Ms. Parrish was one of his classmates. I located a couple other possible classmates, but unfortunately haven't been able to reach them."

Nat smacked him on the back in a congratulatory move. "Your skill amazes me."

He brushed off the praise. "There's more. I'm also looking at Larson's bank records. He gets a direct deposit bi-weekly from his employer, a local cable company. He's one of their installation technicians, who just happened to not show up for work today according to his supervisor. And get this, I found an unusually large withdrawal last week. Like the majority of his savings account was cleared out. It's possible he bought the van with cash, which is why the plates are stolen. So, that's most likely a dead end. I also have his current home address. Our suspect is quite the vagabond. Want to take a guess how often he's moved over the last four years?"

Kurt looked between the two of us expectantly.

I responded with certainty. "I'm gonna go with once every six months."

"Bingo. I pulled up his past residence history and Mr. Larson here has lived within two blocks of each and every one of our victims. I don't know if he moved and then found his victims or if he found his victims and then moved. But I do know he certainly wasn't Mr. Rogers and I wouldn't want to be his neighbor."

Nat cursed. "Son of a bitch. What about his skill with computers? You're the one who said this guy was good. He's a cable technician for fuck's sake. How does someone like that get the type of hacking skills that give you trouble?"

Kurt leaned back in his chair arms crossed. "By getting his Master's degree in computer science with a minor in cyber security from Stanford."

"What the fuck is a computer science geek, no offense, doing working at a cable company?" I queried in confusion.

"Opportunity, maybe? I mean, working as a cable technician gives him the perfect opportunity to enter people's homes at anytime. He can show up to their door and tell them there's a cable outage in the area and he needs to check to make sure everything is working properly. Believe it or not, there are people who would actually let someone like that into their house. Some of them don't know the difference. And, if he's in a real uniform with a real company truck in their driveway, it's easy. Neighbors spotting the truck would assume the resident had called the company for a repair. It's actually pretty genius, if you ask me."

"So, we have opportunity. What about motive?"

"Sorry, that I can't help you with. Out of my area of expertise."

"We know you're doing the best you can. We're just frustrated because there isn't much we can do at this point."

Kurt nodded in commiseration. "I totally get it. I promise you though, we're all working as hard as we can to find your woman. If I were you two, I'd be feeling the same impotent rage at being unable to do anything for the woman I loved. Try not to worry. We'll find her for you guys."

My eyes darted to Nat's in surprise. We'd never mentioned our proclivity of sharing women to anyone in the agency. Not that we were ashamed, it just wasn't anyone's business. Although really, our level of fear and commitment to finding Madeline was obviously a clue to what she meant to us. Or at least to one of us. But for Kurt to make the automatic assumption was telling.

"Thanks, man. We appreciate all the hard work everyone is putting in to find Madeline. I know I haven't been the nicest person to work with."

This admission from Nat didn't surprise me. He'd become less angry and volatile since Madeline came into our lives. Darkness continued to reside inside him, most obvious in his sexual play, but occasionally a sliver of light peeked out.

Kurt just shrugged. "Honestly, you're not the worst dickhead I've ever worked with. Don't worry about it man."

Just then, his computer pinged, and he spun around in his

chair to return to his keyboard. We assumed there was nothing more we could do at this point, so we turned to leave.

"Text us Larson's address will ya? We're gonna see about getting a court order to enter the premises."

"Guys, you probably want to stick around," he threw over his shoulder. "I think I have something."

Turning on the balls of our feet, we raced back to Kurt's desk looking over his shoulder at the large 35" monitor, one of many displayed around the room.

"I sent out an APB on a 1997 GMC Savana Cargo Van as well as the plate number. I just got a hit from a State Trooper who says he spotted the van entering the George Washington and Jefferson National Forests near Goshen, Virginia about two hours ago. He radioed in for an unmarked car and they followed them until he turned off of an old service road no longer in operation outside Hot Springs, Virginia."

Nat stood from his leaned over position. "What the fuck? The Washington and Jefferson is four hours from here. Why there? Does he know where the service road ends? Or what's at the end of it?"

"He said there's nothing at the end of it. There used to be one of several working hot springs that kids would sneak out to, but it's long since dried up. It's barren forest out there."

I shook my head completely disagreeing. "No. There's something out there. Otherwise why would he take her there? Think about every note Casanova has written to his victims. He's in love with them. The whole purpose of each of those letters is to let them know they belong together, and that he's coming for them. Think about it. Every last letter those women received before being killed were ones of anger that she wasn't who he thought she was. I really believe that in his head, those women were a substitute. At least until he found the real Madeline. She's been his target all along. Now he has her. And he's expecting her to love him back. There's always been a desperate tone to his notes when it comes to her loving him like he loves her."

Nat pondered my words. "You're right. Madeline is smart too. She's been studying this guy for months. Knows how he thinks. What makes him tick. She's going to play along with him, placate him, get inside his head and know exactly how to act and respond. She also trusts us to find her, which means she's going to do everything she can to stay alive."

Kurt turned in his chair, stood, and reached into his desk drawer, withdrawing a Glock 9mm standard issue gun, surprising the hell out of us.

Who knew the IT geek could handle a weapon?

"What are we waiting for? Let's go get your woman and bring an end to this piece of shit."

His words startled us into action and we raced out of the office, Kurt keeping up with us every step of the way.

CHAPTER 26

adeline

"GRADY, LISTEN TO ME. YOU'RE STRONGER THAN HIM. DON'T LET him take over. Fight. I know you can do this."

He paused for a minute, his face rigid in concentration, like he truly was fighting. Then, his expression changed and insidious, mocking laughter fell from the demonic smile crossing his face, and he took several more steps closer. "Give it up, Doc. Grady is gone. I'm the one in charge now. I'm going to enjoy cutting your heart out and fucking that sweet pussy of yours. That's one thing I never did with my other girls. They were pure, unlike you. You like the feel of a cock inside you."

I almost vomited at his words. Then it hit me. I was a brilliant psychologist who knew what the fuck I was doing when it came to my patients. If anyone saw me now and what I was prepared to do, they'd think I'd lost it. But there was no way in hell, I was going out like this. Not when I hadn't exhausted all my options yet. Armed with a pair of brass balls courtesy of watching

Nathaniel in action, I drew upon some inner strength and started to laugh. I laughed and laughed until I was almost hysterical. Which was my whole intent since Bad Grady stopped short. I wiped away faux tears.

I sneered up at him, my expression twisted into one of disdain. "You're so fucking worthless. Even your dad thought so. That's why you killed him isn't it? He knew what a sad and sorry piece of shit you are. You think you're some bad ass, whatever your name is, but deep down inside you're still the little pussy who gets pushed around on the playground. Deep down, you're still Grady. You're that pitiful kid who got bullied and had to have a girl put your bully in his place, because you were too scared to do it. You can come up with however many alters you want to make yourself feel better, Grady, but you'll always be useless. Your father was right. You never should have been born."

It was like every molecule had been sucked from the room, the air was so still. I wanted to keep egging him on, but I'd just dealt a mocking blow, and I needed to see what the outcome would be first. I didn't want to push too hard and sever the connection between Grady and Jordan. Besides, I had no idea how many alters I might be dealing with. As I watched though, there was such a long pause with no backlash that I wondered if 'Jordan' was dissociating again and a new alter, or Grady, was going to appear.

"Shut the fuck up," Jordan, or whoever was now present, screeched, spittle spraying from his lips in his rage. "You have no idea what you're talking about."

I'd clearly pushed a button. Dissociative Identity Disorder was not my area of expertise, and the study of the topic had evolved so much since I was in school. However, the roots of the disorder were static. History of childhood physical, emotional, sexual abuse, or PTSD. In Grady's case I didn't know which of those made up his psychosis, but regardless, based on this reaction regarding his father, I knew I'd hit it on the mark.

"You and I both know I'm right, don't we, Jordan? Poor Grady had to create you to cope with the abuse you suffered from your father, but deep down, you *are* Grady and he's you. Your father still beat the shit out of you. Maybe even touched you."

Jordan covered his head with his hands, shaking it back and forth, his face distorted like he was pain. He began to mumble, his voice gaining strength until eventually he was loudly berating himself. It was weirdly fascinating to watch the interaction. I knew that the true conversations were going on inside Grady's head, but to see them manifesting themselves externally was something I'd never experienced before. My clinical side wanted to study him, which was totally fucked up considering the circumstances.

I was so distracted by my own thoughts, that I didn't realize the room had gone silent. My gaze darted to Jordan, who now sat with glazed over eyes, like he was lost in the memories.

"The first time it happened, I was ten. I'd missed the bus coming home from school. It wasn't my fault. One of the boys in my class had hidden my backpack. I spent forever looking for it, so by the time I found it, the bus had already left. My dad was so mad. He'd had to leave work to come pick me up, because the school couldn't get a hold of my mom." His recitation was monotone and completely devoid of any emotion. It was creepy as hell. It was like he was telling me someone else's story. I also recognized that, for the moment, Grady was back. There was the lost little boy quality to him.

"Your dad hit you." It wasn't a question.

He gave a self-deprecating laugh. One that was utterly hollow sounding. "Hit me is putting it mildly. He beat the shit out of me. Cracked a couple ribs. I was left with black and blue bruises for weeks. All under my clothes though. He never hit me where anyone could see."

"Why didn't your mom stop him?"

Finally, he glanced at me. "For someone who's so smart, you're kind of dumb. My mother was your typical abused spouse. She tried to protect me the best she could, but most often got a black eye for her trouble."

It was no wonder he had set me so high up on this pedestal of his. I'd stuck up for him. Something even his mother hadn't done for him. Not really.

I was hesitant to ask my next question, but I wanted answers and knew Grady would be the only one willing to provide them. "When did Jordan show up?"

"After you left Mill Valley."

There was so much accusation in his response it was like a punch to the gut. It left no doubt that Grady blamed me entirely for his disorder, even as he continued to profess his love for me all these years. Why he sent me all those letters. Yet, I was still curious.

"Is there anyone else in there?" I gestured to his head.

He shook his head. "Just Jordan. He's getting stronger though Madeline. He's staying the primary alter for longer and longer periods of time."

I wasn't surprised by his admission. "He's staying longer because you're letting him, Grady You continue to put yourself in situations that make him want to return. You've been living with this DID for, what, twenty-five years? You know how the disorder works."

He collapsed into the chair, his shoulders slumped and head hung in defeat. "I know, but I don't know what to do."

"You have to turn yourself in. You've killed five women, Grady. Jordan may have been the alter present at the time, but they're still going to blame you. The good thing is, you'll get the help you need. It's the only way to stay in control and save lives. You're stronger than he is. You can do this."

I sat in silence, waiting, praying while he continued to sit in what I hoped was contemplative silence. Then, his shoulders stiffened and he sat up straight.

Proud.

L.K. SHAW

Strong.

Then he nodded like he'd made a decision. "Let's call in your boyfriends."

I sagged in relief and barely held back the sob of happiness. "Thank you, Grady. You're doing the right thing."

His smile was a little sad as he rose from his chair. He held out a hand, one that, no matter what decision he'd just made, I was reluctant to take. In a show of good faith, I placed my hand in his. I screamed when he jerked me toward him, spinning me around and trapping my back against his front. A burning pain spread across my neck. I struggled, even as I could feel a warmth running down my chest.

"Stupid bitch," Jordan spat against my cheek, the bloodied knife flashing in front of my face. "Did you really think I was going to go away that easily? You said yourself how worthless Grady was. I can't believe how fucking gullible you were to think that you could bring that pussy back so easily. Please. Grady's gone. I'm the one in charge now. Can you feel your heart pounding? That rush of fucking adrenaline?"

I could hear his voice, but I couldn't make out his words while I gasped for air. My hand went to my throat and found wetness there. He hadn't sliced an artery, but I was still bleeding profusely. My body was in shock. I couldn't fight. I was completely numb.

"I've wanted to see you bleed for months, Madeline. The sight of it now spreading across your shirt makes me hungry for more."

Jordan ground his pelvis against my ass, his erection telling me exactly what he was hungry for. Bile rose in my throat, burning a path upward, but I swallowed it down. The pain in my neck truly registered, and tears scorched a path down my cheeks. I didn't want to die like this.

Still holding me against him, he propelled us forward toward the hallway that I presumed led to a bedroom. The synapses in my brain finally started firing, because my fight mechanism kicked in and some of the self-defense moves my friend, Connor, had

162

taught me suddenly came to mind. My body went completely limp and while I collapsed, I grabbed Jordan's forearms, breaking his hold on me. The minute my knee hit the floor I drove an elbow upward into his groin. He hunched forward in agony. I jumped to my feet and with both fists gripped together to form a club, I used all my force and momentum to bash my hands against the side of his head. I turned and raced for the door, throwing it open and rushing outside.

Not wanting to waste any precious seconds, I took off down the driveway and headed toward where I thought I remembered the road being. It was the middle of the night and even with the full moon shining down, visibility was limited. I stumbled on the rocks, but thankfully kept my balance, but just barely.

"There's nowhere to go, Madeline," Jordan roared from somewhere behind me. My pace didn't slow and I didn't look back. Arms pumping, heart racing, I sucked in lungfuls of air as I sprinted as fast as I could. I had no idea where I was and I warred with myself. Did I stay on the road and hope for a car to possibly come by, even though the chances were slim to none given how late it was and the fact we seemed to be in the middle of nowhere? Common sense told me to try and hide in the forest until morning light and then make my escape. The decision was made for me when I spotted the brightening lights coming from around the curve in the road and the sound of a vehicle.

I began waving my arms wildly. "Help! Please, help me!"

Suddenly, the wind was knocked out of me as I was tackled from behind. My vision blackened when my head slammed against the concrete.

"You fucking cunt." I could barely make out the words from the ringing in my ears. "I'm gonna cut your fucking heart out of your chest."

"Freeze! Put down the knife. Now."

I turned my head but quickly squeezed my eyes shut when the glare of headlights almost blinded me.

"I said, put the knife down. Or don't, because I'd really like to put a bullet in your Goddamn brain."

The concussion I most likely had must be making me hear things, because I could have sworn that was Nathaniel's voice.

"Angel, are you okay?"

I whimpered and choked back a sob. I wasn't crazy. Joseph was the only one who called me 'angel.' They were here. My eyes opened and I looked up at Jordan who was straddling my stomach.

"I'm okay," my voice came out shaky and hoarse. God, my throat hurt so bad.

The white of the headlights illuminated his features. The knife was clutched tightly in his fist and rested on his thigh. I could see his muscles twitch like he was resisting any movement. He was looking down at me with so many emotions it was overpowering. Behind the hatred, I also saw love. Mostly, though, I saw sadness and defeat. Jordan knew that it was over. His face then became expressionless and he zoned out. I knew he was dissociating.

He blinked and focused his gaze back on me. Grady had returned. He looked down at the knife, then up at my men, then back toward me. His expression shifted to something undefinable.

"I'm sorry. For everything," he whispered, his voice breaking.

It all happened so fast. Grady roared, raised the knife now clutched in both fists in the air, and I flinched, my eyes slamming shut as I prepared for death. Gunshots sounded and I felt his entire body jerk and twitch. My eyes flew open and his body was frozen, a pained expression on his face. The knife fell from his upraised hands, metal clattering against the pavement, the sound coming loudly from next to my ear. I could only watch as dark, crimson spots formed on his clothes, growing larger with each passing second.

Shuffling noises drew my attention and then Grady's body tumbled sideways off mine. Gentle hands lifted me off the ground and soon I was cradled in Nathaniel's arms. Still, I couldn't look away from the man lying on the ground. He stared up at me with such sadness, his mouth moved soundlessly with the words "I love you." He took in one last shuddering breath and then... nothing.

"Jesus, she's bleeding. Get me a cloth or something." Joseph barked out the order as my Nathaniel carried me toward the car. My teeth began to chatter and my whole body shook.

"Fuck, she's going into shock. Kurt, call 9-1-1 now. Joseph, grab my jacket."

Warmth surrounded me as Nathaniel climbed into the backseat with me still wrapped in his arms. His scent surrounded me when his coat was placed over us. I couldn't control the tremors that wracked my body.

"Shh, pet, don't cry. We've got you. You're safe." I didn't even realize I *was* crying. Since Nathaniel still cradled me, it must have been Joseph brushing my hair off my face. I forced my eyes open to look at him. I needed the reassurance that this wasn't just a dream and that they were truly here. Through blurred vision, he was there like a lifeline waiting to catch me.

"I need to put this on your neck to stop the bleeding." Movement followed his words, and I sucked in a pained breath when he applied pressure to my wound.

"Paramedics are on their way. I also double checked on"— Kurt, if I remembered correctly, paused and nodded his head in the general direction of where Grady's body was—"our deceased."

A flicker of sympathy surfaced. What happened to him wasn't his fault. He'd merely been a victim of circumstance. I had no idea how his mother would feel about his death, but she needed to be notified. I wasn't going to think about that now. It was over. I was safe in the arms of my men. And they were mine. As I was theirs.

My dearest Madeline,

I want to tell you a story. But not just any story. This one is special. It's about a boy. And a girl. One day, this boy was walking through a copse of trees. The smell of rain, and the redwoods surrounding him, tantalized his nose. Sunlight dappled the ground as it peeked through the giant, cinnamon-colored skyscrapers, casting shadows on the hard, dirt floor. And even though he knew the sun was waning, he marched on, patiently, in search of the perfect tree.

Forty minutes passed and still he searched, his eyes scanning the foliage around him. The temperature began to drop and the boy shivered. But he carried on. The wildlife quieted while he trekked through their domain, as if sensing something not quite right. Several pairs of eyes followed the path the boy took, but the owners remained cautious and wary.

And then, there it was, right in front of him. Larger than any tree he had ever seen. Instantly, the boy knew it was the one. Reverently, he walked around the tree, his head tilted back as he scanned the trunk upward, craning his neck until his eyes spotted the pinnacle. It was the perfect spot.

The boy's fingertips caressed the bark, feeling the coolness of it sink into his bones. Suddenly, in his hand was a knife. With careful precision, he began to carve into the tree, his tongue peeking from between his lips as he scratched in deep concentration. Chips dropped to the ground from the damage he inflicted on the tree, but he continued on, until soon, he stepped back and admired his work.

In the reddish-colored wood was now etched a heart, and inside the heart were two small letters separated by a plus sign. Yet, to this little boy, they signified everything. They signified love. The immense emotion that filled him up. His entire existence would forever be a part of that glorious tree. SHE, the girl who owned his heart, would forever be a part of that tree.

Soon the boy grew up, but every so often he'd go visit that tree. His now large fingers would trace the letters reminding him of the love that filled his heart to over-flowing. A love that spanned decades. Finally, the time had come for the man, and now woman, to be together. But as with all things, change is fluid. What once was can no longer be. The man realized this. I realized this. Since you're reading this, Madeline, it must mean that things didn't go as I'd planned. They rarely do, so it really comes as no surprise. Merely another disappointment in life. I can't be sad though. It only means I must wait a little longer for us to be together. Because whatever didn't happen in this life, is surely meant to happen in the next. Until I see you again, know that love transcends heaven and hell.

    All my love,
    Grady

CHAPTER 27

$\mathcal{M}$adeline

EVER SINCE I WAS RELEASED FROM THE HOSPITAL, I'D SPENT EVERY night at Joseph and Nathaniel's. We'd even discussed putting my house on the market. We'd gone to Black Light a few times, but mentally I was still recovering. So, more often than not we played at home. Tonight was one of those nights. I had a special request though that I knew wasn't going to go over well.

"I want you to bring out your knife tonight."

Nathaniel's response was instantaneous. "No fucking way."

I reached out and clasped his hands in mine. He tightened his grip to stop the tremble in my touch. Yes, I was nervous as hell. I still had the occasional nightmare remembering when Jordan sliced my throat, but I needed to do this. The three of us had been together for two months now, and not once, even before Grady, had Nathaniel brought up the discussion of knife play. He'd respected my hard limit from that first night, so I knew he wasn't trying to push me into anything, which I appreciated. But I sensed that he missed his knives.

If I were being honest, I'd done some research on it, and I could admit to being intrigued by the mind fuck behind it. Like a master at the bullwhip, I was sure the knife was like an extension of him and that he was an artist at wielding it. I think the minute I'd begun my research that my hard limit would change to a soft one. Grady had gone and fucked that up. But I refused to let him win. He wasn't going to ruin one more minute of my life. It was time to take back the control he'd stripped from me. Nothing like tonight to take that leap.

"We both need this, Nathaniel. Your knife is a part of who you are as a Dom. You need to wield it, and I need to let you. Grady... Jordan... I won't let them destroy this for us. I trust you, Master. With my life. With my heart. With my submission." I held my breath while I waited for him to relent. It was his job as my Dom to give me what I needed. I'd finally reached a point where I now knew what I needed and could easily express it. It had never been that way with Vince or any of the other Doms I'd scened with. Not true soul-deep needs. But now, I was asking for this. It was probably one of the most important needs I'd ever ask be fulfilled. It was for both of us.

Nathaniel exhaled a large sigh and I knew he was going to agree. "The minute, no the second, something doesn't feel right, I better hear your safe word or you're going to be in for a far greater punishment."

I squeezed his hand tightly. "Thank you, Master. I promise I'll safe word if it becomes too much."

His eyes darkened to pitch and his fingers twitched. "I'll assume the no blood hard limit hasn't changed."

It wasn't a question, but I responded any way so there were no misunderstandings. "Correct. No blood drawn."

"Good, because I don't think I could handle that even though I'm aware of the risks that can potentially, however unintentionally, occur. I've been practicing knife play for years, and am considered an expert. You, however, are not only new to it, but you also have the potential for a traumatic response, so an accident has the potential to happen. However, I will take every caution possible to avoid it, and I have an entire first aid kit available should a cut occur. Are you willing to accept these risks?"

I nodded and repeated my previous words. "I trust you, Master."

"Thank you for that trust, pet. Go with Joseph, and I'll be there in a moment."

Joseph's finger traced down my arm, my skin pebbling in the wake of the path, before clasping my hand in his. "Come."

He led me to his room and had me sit on the edge of the bed. He disappeared out into the hall, but quickly returned. In his hands was a spanking bench.

"You're certainly prepared for anything, aren't you?" I joked.

Joseph grinned. "My mother always taught me to be ready for anything."

We both turned when Nathaniel entered the room. In his hands was a duffel bag. And what looked like a folded up tarp.

I pointed at the plastic with trepidation. "What is that for?"

Nathaniel held it up for my inspection. "Have you ever done wax play?"

"No, but I've watched it done. It looks like it feels wonderful though."

He nodded in Joseph's direction. "I thought it might be a good idea for Joseph to try out his new wax set on you if you're agreeable. It might help your focus."

"Oh, I think that's a great idea." Joseph turned to me. "I've been wanting to decorate your body since that first night. Will you let me, angel?"

My gaze passed between the two of them. The love and trust I felt was all encompassing. I knew they wouldn't do anything to harm me.

"Yes, Master." There was no other answer to give.

"You won't regret it, Madeline."

I remained sitting on the bed while I watched the men spread out the tarp and then place the spanking bench in the middle of it. Joseph winked at me.

"Wax can get a little messy."

I just stared, not sure how to respond.

"You ready, pet?" My gaze darted to Nathaniel who'd placed his bag on the bedside table. I made myself look at it knowing what was inside. I could do this.

"I'm ready, Master."

"Good. Now, strip."

CHAPTER 28

$\mathcal{N}$athaniel

WHILE JOSEPH LED MADELINE OVER TO THE BENCH HE'D BROUGHT in, I pulled out my favorite toy from my bag. A four-inch blade with a custom-made lightweight grip. I also withdrew all of my safety supplies, including antiseptic ointment, butterfly bandages, and skin glue as well as my sanitizing equipment. Over my shoulder I heard Joseph whispering to her, and I turned to see a blush spread across her naked chest, her nipples pebbled with need. She stood proudly, secure in the fact that we found her utterly enchanting. Her light shone so brightly it was almost overpowering. Shaking off my fanciful thoughts, I nodded to Joseph. "Pet, we're going to make all your dreams come true. Dreams you didn't even know you had."

She cocked her head and beamed up at me. "I can't wait, Master."

"Joseph," I called over to him. "Let's show our little submissive here what she's been missing out on."

He and I exchanged places and while he went to get his bag out of his closet, I moved in front of Madeline. I removed the blade from its protective leather sheath, wanting her to see the blade that would be touching her skin. I didn't want her afraid.

"This is my favorite." I held the blade out so she could see it, perhaps admire it as much I did. "The silver complements your violet eyes you know, especially when the light reflects off it. I can't wait to see the tip running across your flawless skin, the shallow markings it leaves behind a reminder to both of us the level of trust you're giving me. I'm humbled by it."

To emphasize my point, I gently ran the dull side down my own arm showing her on my own body before touching her with it. I kept a close eye on her for any signs of distress. I knew there would be fear given what had happened to her, but I wanted no harm, neither physical nor mental, to come to her. When she did nothing more than follow my movements, I removed the knife from my skin and ever so slowly placed the dull side on her arm and mimicked the motion I'd just completed on myself.

I made sure to keep pressure off the upper region and exerted just the slightest more on her forearm, pulling the blade downward. Her eyes followed its path, her pupils dilated with a combination of fear and arousal if her hitched breath was any indication. Her tongue darted out to moisten her lips before she bit down on the bottom one, perhaps to hold back any words of regret for her choice.

Joseph and I wanted everything that happened here tonight to be her choice, and even as an experienced sub, she needed to be reminded of that. "Anytime you no longer feel safe or if something isn't working for you, we want you to use your safe word. There won't be any anger or disappointment for either of us. Your trust in us is the most important thing, so don't be afraid to stop whatever is happening if it doesn't feel good. Understand?"

Madeline nodded, her eyes never leaving mine. "Yes, Master."

Joseph reached into his own bag and withdrew a red and pink

candle as well as a piece of fabric. He'd been dying to decorate Madeline's body from day one, and now it seemed he was about to get his chance.

"Close your eyes," I breathed into Madeline's ear before biting down on it.

Her eyes fluttered and she drew in a shuddering breath before she completely shut her eyes. Joseph handed me the black satin blindfold. I teased her shoulders with it, letting the soft fabric caress her skin. I brushed it across her shoulder blades when I moved behind her. Her body moved with the flow of the cloth, like she was chasing the sensation. I drew the blindfold over the top of her, covering her closed lids, and tying it behind her head, gently but firmly cinching the knot taking care not to catch her hair in it.

"Focus on what your body is feeling. Don't think about anything. Just enjoy the sensations." Joseph gently brushed his finger across her cheek causing Madeline to lean into his touch, almost purring.

"Yes, Master," she breathed out. She was fucking beautiful standing there, blindfolded eyes, completely trusting her Doms to take care of her.

"Next time I want you in clothes so I can cut them off you."

She trembled at my words. Joseph nuzzled her neck while I approached her other side. I knelt at her feet and ran my hands up her legs, leaning in and blowing my hot breath across her pussy. She moaned at the sensation. I continued to caress her, moving closer to her center each time. Her pussy grew wet at my touch. I stood, cupping her in my hand and drawing a finger through her slit, flicking her clit. I slid the digit back down and this time when I got to her pussy I slid inside while I whispered in her ear all the fucked up things we were going to do to her. "Before this night is over you're going to feel the delicious burn of the wax on your skin and the coldness of my blade scraping it off. The shallow marks from my knife will be a reminder in the days to come of being owned by us. Possessed by us. You're going to look at your skin and remember the fear and exhilaration of the bite of the blade. That excites you doesn't it? I can feel your juices flowing faster. Listen to the sound of your wetness beneath my fingers. You're dying to experience the sensations that only we can provide. Can you hear your heart racing? The blood flowing in your veins? I know I can. My cock is harder than it has ever been with just the thought of sliding deep inside this hot, wet pussy. We want to spill our seed deep inside you, marking you as ours. When we're done with you, our come is going to become a part of you."

Madeline's knees almost buckled, but Joseph caught her in his arms.

"On your stomach."

Joseph and I were equal partners when it came to sharing women. He was just as dominant as I was. However, each play was different and we each took the appropriate lead when warranted. Tonight, I was the one leading this scene. Joseph was still fully in control, but we worked in tandem and let the other have full control when it fit our needs at the time. There was no jealousy or fear of being topped. It's why we worked so well together both inside the bedroom and out. We were entirely in sync with each other. We fed off each other's control.

Once Madeline was properly situated over the bench, it was Joseph's turn to lead. I was more than happy to sit back and watch the show until it was my turn again. The smell of a freshly lit match stung my nostrils as the spark brightly lit up the end of the short wooden stick. Joseph touched the burning flame to the candle wick, igniting and sending a faint waxy smell in the air. He let the candle burn for a minute before holding it up and tilting it over his own hand to test the temperature. He must have been satisfied with the heat level because he moved closer to Madeline. I squatted next to her, my finger lining a path down her arm, so she remained physically connected to one of us.

When he tilted the candle over her back, she gasped at the feel of the heated wax dripping onto her skin.

"What color, pet?"

"Green, Master. I can feel the warmth flowing through me."

I nodded up at Joseph for him to continue. This time instead of my finger, I used the dull edge of my blade to caress the skin of her forearm. Just when I withdrew from her, Joseph poured more wax from the candle, drawing a line across her. We repeated our movements, me moving the blade lightly across various areas of her skin in opposition to Joseph decorating her body with his colored wax. With each drop, Madeline moaned her pleasure, although I could tell the effort it took her not to flinch and squirm.

"Still green, Madeline?"

"Yes, Master," came her drowsy reply. Shock coursed through me. She was definitely close to subspace, and hadn't once flinched or tried to draw away from the touch of the blade. We stopped periodically, caressing her body, Joseph with his fingers, and me with my knife. I scratched shallow marks on her inner thighs, careful to not scrape too deep. Before long, the most gorgeous array of red and pink splashes colored her porcelain skin.

I caressed her ass, my fingers catching on the raised wax dashed across her cheeks. Gently, I inched my blade under the first batch of wax, prying it off her skin, the pink of her flesh standing out against the silver metal. Once the piece had been scraped off, Joseph bent down and licked the area now absent of wax. Piece by piece I used my knife to remove every bit of wax while Joseph nibbled and kissed each exposed inch of her. Once her back and ass had returned to complete bare nakedness, I leaned down to whisper encouragement.

"I'm so proud of you pet. Not once did you flinch at the touch of the blade."

Madeline nodded lazily, a happy smile of content on her face. I removed the blindfold, pushing her hair out of her face. Her eyes were glazed over when she peered up at me and I knew she was flying high. I helped her off the bench and with arms under her knees and behind her back, I picked her up, cuddling her close to my chest as I carried her to the bed. Joseph took a seat and I sat next to him, our sub sitting on my lap. He placed her feet over his thighs and began to rub and massage her feet and legs while I rubbed the arm clutching my shirt. Madeline rested her head against my shoulder, her nose buried in my neck. I lost complete track of time while we provided aftercare to our sub. I couldn't remember ever feeling this close connection to a sub before. I wasn't ready for it to end.

Finally, she shifted in our embrace, stretching and arching like a cat.

"Welcome back, pet."

She drowsily smiled, a sigh of contentment coming from her. "That was amazing. Thank you Master for sharing that experience with me."

Joseph squeezed her thigh. "Oh, love, the night isn't over yet."

adeline

LAST NIGHT HAD BEEN INCREDIBLE. NATHANIEL AND JOSEPH HAD been so patient with me. I'd used my clinical skills and every breathing technique and positive thinking task I'd ever assigned to any of my patients. It had helped me tremendously to get over my fear of the knife. Also, not having to see it against my skin had been a relief. I didn't have to think about it then. I only concentrated on my Doms' voices, their soothing tone keeping me calm and in control.

Once I'd recovered from subspace, they'd taken their time and actually made love to me. I could feel the love in every kiss and every touch. Their whispered words of love settled deep inside my heart. Never before had I felt such peace and happiness. This was what I'd been missing my whole life. These two men. I shifted and stretched. The shallow scratches on my inner thighs and breasts burned hotly. I still shuddered at the sensation of the razor-sharp blade running across my skin. Never in a million years did I think the feel of steel would be such a combination of turn on and terrifying. The thought of the icy coldness of the blade had my blood powering through my veins again, my heart racing in fear and excitement even though the knife had long been put away and I was lying in bed alone. The high was unlike anything else. Knowing that with the wrong move the sharp edge could slice my skin at a moment's notice gave me a rush like an addict after their latest fix.

I rose from the bed and headed to the bathroom. While I washed my breasts and thighs, I paused, my fingers moving over the marks on my body, but not lingering. I quickly dried myself off but stood for a moment staring at my reflection. My gaze traveled up and down my body stopping to admire the same marks I'd ignored a few minutes ago. Marks left by Nathaniel and his knife. They were beautiful in their raw and primal state. Each one burned into my skin like a permanent brand he'd left behind. A brand that signified I belonged to him. My heart thumped a thousand times a minute at the thought.

Dressing quickly, I headed downstairs. I lingered at the edge of the doorway, watching, admiring Joseph and Nathaniel standing there, working together as a team making breakfast. Always together. Joseph caught sight of me first. There was so much love on his face at seeing me.

"Good morning, angel." He greeted me with a kiss on the lips.

"Morning."

"Pet." Nathaniel brushed his lips across his favorite spot, my forehead. "Sit. Breakfast is almost ready."

I took my usual place and drank some of my juice. Soon, we were all sitting together. The pancakes were perfect. "Mmm. These are so good. I can never get mine this fluffy. They're always flat and rubbery. I could eat these every day." I moaned again in appreciation of the deliciousness.

"Man, that is high praise. I can only hope they always live up to your high standards."

I stuck my tongue out at him.

"Careful pet. I can find a much better use for that tongue if you aren't careful." There was a teasing twinkle in Nathaniel's eye.

"How are you feeling this morning?"

I looked at Joseph. "Happy."

"I'm so glad. We were also hoping to make you happier."

My hand reached out to clutch his. "You've already made me the happiest woman ever. I know I haven't said it yet, but I love you, Joseph."

I grabbed Nathaniel's hand and my eyes bored directly into his, staring deep into his soul. "And I love you, Nathaniel. More than I've ever loved anyone before. The two of you are the other parts of my heart. Before I met you, I was miserable. I thought there was something wrong with me. That I was unworthy of the love of a Dom. You both showed me how wrong I was. You showed me what I'd been missing in my life. You were what was missing."

Joseph released my hand and rose from the table. My eyes followed his movements as he disappeared upstairs. I sent a worried look to Nathaniel who only squeezed my hand tighter and smiled at me. Footsteps sounded and I turned back to see him descending the stairs with a box in his hand. The man beside me moved, tugging my hand to turn me in my chair. I covered my mouth with my hand and held back the tears when I spotted Nathaniel on his knees. His best friend soon joined him.

"Madeline, from the moment I first spotted you at Black Light wearing that little white dress with those too-big glasses framing your face, I knew you were the one. My angel. Even this guy here, the stubborn ass who didn't believe in fate, knew. There's never been a more perfect woman, a perfect submissive, for us. You're everything we've ever needed or wanted. We've been holding on to this since the day you were taken from us. Both of us, even then, were convinced that we were all meant to be together."

Joseph opened the box. Inside lay the most beautiful collar. It was a rose gold choker chain. But what made it special was that the chain was threaded through three hearts, each one a different color. White, yellow, and rose signifying each of us. It was absolutely stunning and brought tears to my eyes.

"Madeline, pet, will you accept our collar?"

I nodded fiercely and dropped to my knees with them, throwing my arms around their necks and pulling them close to me. Their warm arms embraced me and the three of us sat there, intertwined, connected, the way we were meant to be.

The End

ABOUT THE AUTHOR

LK Shaw is a physical therapist assistant by day and author/social media addict by night. She resides in South Carolina with her high maintenance beagle mix dog, Miss P, who should probably just have her own Instagram account. An avid reader since childhood, she became hooked on historical romance novels in high school. She now reads, and loves, all romance sub-genres, with erotic romance and romantic suspense being her favorite. LK enjoys traveling and chocolate. Her books feature hot alpha heroes and the strong women they love.

LK loves to interact with readers. You can follow her on any of her social media. Don't forget to sign up for her monthly newsletter! http://eepurl.com/ds5MOb

Make sure to follow LK for more new releases coming soon!

BLACK COLLAR PRESS

Did you enjoy your visit to Black Light? Have you read the other books in the series?

Infamous Love, A Black Light Prequel by Livia Grant
Black Light: Rocked by Livia Grant
Black Light: Exposed by Jennifer Bene
Black Light: Valentine Roulette by Various Authors
Black Light: Suspended by Maggie Ryan
Black Light: Cuffed by Measha Stone
Black Light: Rescued by Livia Grant
Black Light: Roulette Redux by Various Authors
Complicated Love, A Black Light Novel
Black Light: Suspicion by Measha Stone
Black Light: Obsessed by Dani Rene
Black Light: Fearless by Maren Smith
Black Light: Possession by LK Shaw

Black Collar Press is a small publishing house started by authors Livia Grant and Jennifer Bene in late 2016. The purpose was simple - to create a place where the erotic, kinky, and exciting worlds they love to explore could thrive and be joined by other like-minded authors.

If this is something that interests you, please go to the Black Collar Press website and read through the FAQs. If your questions are not answered there, please contact us directly at: blackcollarpress@gmail.com.

WHERE TO FIND BLACK COLLAR PRESS:

- Website: http://www.blackcollarpress.com/
- Facebook: https://www.facebook.com/blackcollarpress/
- Twitter: https://twitter.com/BlackCollarPres

DON'T MISS MORE ROULETTE FUN

Coming February 7th, 2019

Black Light: Celebrity Roulette

Join us for our third installment of naughty fun. The party has moved to the West Coast club this year with nine brand new stories... nine brand new couples... and hours of reading pleasure.

Stories by: Jennifer Bene, Livia Grant, Renee Rose, Sue Lyndon, Maren Smith, Measha Stone, Dani Rene, Maggie Ryan and Lesley Clark.

Mark your Calendar!